IAN WISBY

THE

HEAD OF STATE

THE HEAD OF STATE

Copyright © 2021 by Ian Wisby

THE HEAD OF STATE

All rights reserved. No part of this book may be used or reproduced in any manner whatsoever without written permission except in the case of brief quotations embodied in critical articles or reviews.

This book is a work of fiction. Names, characters, businesses, organisations, places, events, and incidents either are the product of the author's imagination or are used fictitiously. Any resemblance to actual persons, living or dead, events, or locales is entirely coincidental.

ISBN-13: 9798700348607

Imprint: Independently Published

I'd like to dedicate this book to my family.

Thank you for being so supportive.

Prologue

The shrill sound that woke Angela Shaw must have been from hell. She had been in the middle of a dream that put a big smile on her face. She didn't remember what the dream was as she woke up with a start. *Damn alarm!* She groaned seconds before realizing it was not her alarm. It was her partner's phone. The ring tone was the Rolling Stones' Sympathy for The Devil song. Now, it was a shrilling tune that had stolen her sweet sleep. She cursed again under her breath as she stirred. Angela hated mornings. She was never one to be woken up early, especially if it was unnecessary. She loved her sleep and cherished every minute she could to use it for sleep. Her husband, Andrew Shaw, answered the call. 'Hello?' His usually gruff voice had an extra edge to it this morning. He hated to be woken from sleep this way. 'My God…Are you sure?' said Andrew. There was a brief pause in the conversation and Andrew closed his eyes. 'Okay, sure. I'll be there as soon as I can. Thank you,' he said, and then hung up. Angela Shaw's eyes widened as her husband broke the news to her.

'Sweetheart, what's wrong?' asked Angela, as she sat up and leaned against her pillow.

'It's Mum…She died early this morning,' he replied.

'Oh sweetheart, I'm so sorry. Come here,' said Angela. She grabbed onto Andrew and held him tightly. She knew how much Andrew loved his mother, but sadly, she had been unwell lately, and it would seem her illness had caught up with her. More than a few times, she had caught herself wishing she had a father she could love that way. Angela's father, John Bradley, was the Spouse of Charmaine Bradley. Angela had recently found out that her mother had been selected to be the nation's first female head of state. She rarely spoke with her mother, as they'd had a huge argument many years ago, over something so stupid, countries would go to war over. One of the reasons that she never spoke with her mother was because of the fact that Angela Shaw was an investigative journalist. Her mother disapproved of the idea of her becoming a journalist, but Angela decided to disobey her mother, and chose to follow her own dream. Angela was a brilliant investigative journalist and had written some award-winning stories. She worked for the Capital Gazette, an independent news and print media house that was struggling to keep up with all the mainstream publishers. But since Angela had started working for them, they'd gained a bit of reputation back. She knew in the back of her head that the only reason they were doing so well was because of her mother, and her recent spike in publicity. It was ever since her mother had been selected to be Australia's first President; everyone seemed to be wanting to hire Angela, but she stuck with the Gazette. Angela never knew what to say in these sorts of situations. She always felt awkward and that if she'd said the wrong thing, it could end up in tears. She reached across to him on the bed and held him tight. The smell of the mint hair oil he used for his hair made her want to kiss him desperately, but she knew that moment wasn't right for it. She held him to herself as the spasms rocked his body. It was just after six thirty in the morning. Normally, Angela would be wide awake hours ago, but she'd been working tirelessly lately, and she needed sleep. 'Are you going to the funeral?' asked Angela, as she slowly got out of bed to get ready for a busy day at work.

'Yeah, I'm catching the next plane out to Melbourne…You want to tag along?' he asked. He knew that she'd say no because Angela was so dedicated to her career. Which he fully respected.

'I wish I could sweetheart, and I am truly sorry about your mother…But we're pushing for a deadline on a major story. This could be the biggest break the Gazette has ever had,' Angela said, icily. Andrew slowly nodded, reluctantly.

'It's okay, I completely understand…Besides, my sister will be a mess, so I'll have to babysit her,' he replied.

'Of course, Sonia.' Angela knew Sonia very well. She was a bit of an alcoholic, and she knew too well that Andrew will have his hands full with that. 'Good luck with that one, sweetheart,' she said, sarcastically.

'Fuck, today is going to be a long day,'

Andrew cursed, as he too got out of bed. He wiped away a tear and headed straight into the bathroom to take a shower. Sonia was Andrew's younger sister. Recently, she'd gone through a tough divorce with her husband. It hit her pretty hard, as she found out her husband had been cheating on her with a secretary at his work. Since then, Sonia had gone through several mental breakdowns, which both saw her end up in hospital as a result of her drinking excessively. She'd always looked up to Andrew, and he always knew what to say and do when she was going through one of her episodes. Angela and Sonia never saw eye to eye. From the day they met when she and Andrew started dating, Sonia was convinced that Angela was out to take him away from her. Meanwhile, Angela had gotten dressed. She then wandered into the kitchen. It was a modern kitchen with all the latest appliances. The house itself was very modern; it came with one of those voice activated 'Home Assistants'. As soon as Angela entered the kitchen, the lights turned on. The coffee machine kicked in and began making a cappuccino. While the coffee was brewing, the flat screen TV switched on. A news report was being displayed and the anchors were talking about the recent incident that took place at the National Press Club in Canberra. Angela's mother, Charmaine Bradley, was shot during her speech at the National Press Club. The speech was to commemorate her success for being selected as Australia's first President. The reporters were stating that a gunman disguised as a waiter had concealed a weapon and used it to attempt to kill Ms. Bradley. They stated that the shooter had been detained by the AFP and was being questioned. They also said that Charmaine Bradley had survived the gunshot and had been in hospital recovering. Angela went over to the kitchen bench and switched on her laptop. She was currently working on a major story, one that would take her career to the next level. It was also a very risky story, but she didn't care. Angela opened up her email inbox. She had dozens of unread emails, but there was one at the top that she'd not read. It was marked as *URGENT* She opened it and carefully read what was in it. The email was sent from a contact of hers. It stated that he wanted to meet with her today, as he'd gotten some more information for her story. Attached to the email were several images. She opened them, and they were images of two murders. She gasped at the sight of them almost dropping her coffee cup. She'd seen this sort of thing before, but she just wasn't expecting this. She looked closely at the photos. The bodies had been brutally murdered. A man and a woman. It would seem she was onto something BIG. Suddenly, her smartphone started ringing. It made her jump as she was too involved with the images on her screen. Angela loved this stuff. She quickly answered the call. 'Hello?'

'It's me. Are you coming in today?' It was Angela's assistant, Sherie.

'Yeah, I'll be there soon. Just getting ready…What's up?'

'The boss wants to see you,' said Sherie. Angela's eyes narrowed. She began to worry.

'What does he want?'

'I don't know, just he wants you in soon.' Angela let out a sigh and closed her eyes.

'Okay…Fine, I'm on my way.' She hung up and closed the lid of her laptop. She thought for a moment, before standing up and collecting her bag from the side table. 'I'm heading out now, sweetheart! Love you!' she called out. Of course, there was no response, just the sound of the shower running. She wondered if she should go in today. She didn't want to leave Andy here by himself, especially in his current condition. But she had to follow this lead up.

She wrote him a quick note and stuck it on the fridge before heading out the door.

14

Angela knew she had to go into work. But it wasn't where she was heading. She had to meet with this contact. He was a very valuable source of information. He was a whistleblower. He was in fact helping Angela build a story that would bring down a major corporate business, one that was corrupt and powerful, and too dangerous to be kept in operation. Angela was seeking to destroy them from the ground up. Whatever it took, she was prepared to do it. Angela was driving her car into the city. She was to meet with her contact at a secret location. She found a parking spot and then headed into Bowen Park, one of Canberra's most popular recreational parks. It sat on the edge of Lake Burley Griffin and just up the road from Parliament House. There were a few people walking through the park. Most were walking their dogs while others were jogging before heading into work. Angela made her way into the park. She arrived at a green bench. The one where she was told to be at. Her contact was very secretive and cloak and dagger style, which was perfectly understandable. It's likely this 'corporation' was behind the two murders. Angela approached the bench. No one was around. There was, however, a man sitting on the far end of the bench. He was reading the newspaper, trying to be inconspicuous. Angela sat down on the opposite side of him. She sat there waiting. Nothing was said between them. She proceeded to take out her phone and pretend to be checking her social media sites. 'Were you followed?' a muffled voice finally spoke.

'Of course not. I was careful. As usual,' Angela replied. 'What's going on?'

'You get those images?'

'Yes. Is this BMC?' the man didn't reply straight away. Angela looked over and saw that he'd lowered his paper.

'I can't say for sure, but it's certainly possible…They were both employees of BMC. It turns out they were also trying to blow the whistle on these guys.'

'Shit. This is big Ken…Who were they?'

'They were senior administration. One was Jennifer Sanders, a private secretary. The other was Ezra Wellington, he worked as a private security consultant. They knew a lot that could do some serious damage,' said Ken. 'It appears that Ezra was working with Jennifer to bring these people down. Ezra contacted me and said he found out something horrible, that BMC were plotting something major to take place in Sydney.'

'Bloody hell…So, you're saying BMC murdered these guys to keep them from talking to the media?'

'It looks that way. They would've used their professional guys. A hit squad if you will…There's something else…I got the name of a witness to the murders.'

'Son of a bitch…Where is this guy?'

'He's in a secure location. But he won't come out until you can guarantee his protection.'

'You know I can't guarantee that. I'm a journalist, not a detective, Ken,' said Angela.

'Yes, but you have people in high places,' he replied. Angela knew who he was talking about. Her mother.

'I can't take this to my mother, Ken. To start with, we're not on talking terms. Secondly, I can't guarantee she'll be able to protect him either.'

'Look, this guy is witness to two homicides, carried out by a hitman. These guys are serious,

Angela,' said Ken. Angela let out a sigh of frustration.

'Okay, look. I can't guarantee success, but I'll see what I can do. As long as I have assurances that this guy is willing to go on the record with everything,' said Angela. Ken didn't say anything at first. He then looked over at Angela with a gentle nod.

'You have it.' Angela smiled, and she knew this story would make her the most famous journalist in Australia.

But once she published this story, she knew it would also make her the most wanted person. Angela Shaw was followed. A dark-coloured vehicle, possibly with fake number plates, was parked just up from Angela's car. There were two men inside and were shielded by the dark tinted windows. One of the men had a large camera. He was snapping photos of Angela Shaw talking with Ken. He then took several more of her getting into her car. He turned to his partner in the driver's seat and nodded. He started up the car and began to follow Angela.

****

After meeting with her contact, Angela Shaw drove across town. She finally arrived at her office. The Capital Gazette was busy as usual. Her fellow colleagues were already hard at work writing on their next best story. Phones were ringing off the hook, and fingernails could be heard tapping away at keyboards. Angela bravely walked down the centre of the main office. She headed towards her boss's office, the Editor-in-Chief. He was currently talking on the phone and she gently knocked on the glass door. He looked up to signal her to come in. 'Yes, of course. I'll make sure it's done today. Alright. Talk later.' He hung up. 'Glad you could make it, Shaw,' he said, bluntly.

'Look, boss. I'm sorry I'm late. I had a

meeting with a contact of mine. I've got a major lead on this story.'

'That's what you've been saying for the past two months, but yet you've dragged up nothing of significance,' he said.

'Brian, don't be like this. My contact is risking his life to get me this information…He's got a witness to a double homicide carried out by a hitman employed by this corporation,' she explained. She then showed Brian the images she received on the email. He looked at them but didn't seem impressed.

'All I see is two dead bodies…Where's the story Angela?'

'Look, these BODIES were employees of BMC. They were murdered because they were on the verge of going public with the story…the story you're denying me,' she said. Brian paused for a moment and looked down at the pictures again.

'So, you're saying that this corporation,

Birchall McClelland, were behind these murders?' he asked. Angela didn't reply straight away.

'It's highly possible, yes…These guys are criminals…My contact said they are corrupt and extremely powerful…He said they're likely financing a terrorist organisation.'

'That's a pretty radical accusation, Shaw,' said Brian.

'I know. But this guy, Ken Marshall, is solid. He assured me the witness is prepared to come forward and testify against these people,' she replied. 'Please, Brian…Give me one more chance…I'm on the verge of breaking through with this story…As soon as this guy talks, BMC are going down. Then you can do whatever you want with me.' Brian wasn't sure about this. He knew that Angela was taking a bit risk with this. But he also knew she was a good journalist, and even if he'd said no, she would just go behind his back.

'Okay fine. I'm giving you twenty-four-hours to get this guy to come forward. After that, I'm pulling the plug, understand?' he said. Angela didn't reply straight away.

'Understood.' She then turned and headed to the door. Before she left, Brian called out to her.

'Listen, Shaw…Be careful,' he said. She smiled.

'I will.' Then she headed back to her desk. Angela was excited. Now that she'd gotten approval from the Editor-in-Chief, she could go into journalistic mode and craft the perfect story. First, she had to find a way to get the witness to come forward and testify. She sat down at her desk and continued to write up what she already had. It was going to be a front page news story, so it had to be engaging. She sat there at her computer. She looked up to see one of the TV screens was showing a news report on the republican referendum. It was also showing a live interview with Charmaine

Bradley, Angela's mother, and her thoughts on being selected to be the nation's first female President. Just then, she was startled. Her phone was ringing. She hesitated for a moment before answering it. 'Angela Shaw?' she answered.

'Hey, Angie. How's my number one daughter?' it was her father, John Bradley. She smiled when she heard his voice.

'Hey Dad. I'm doing great, just at work.'

'I see…Look, I won't keep you. I just wanted to see how you were doing. Your mother is worried about you,' said John.

'Ugh, I'd like to believe that…I saw the news, she must be thrilled.'

'Yes, we are…Are you coming to the Australia Day ceremony?' he asked, cautiously. Angela just closed her eyes and let out a sigh.

'I'm not sure yet Dad. I'll see how I go. I may have to work that day.'

'Come on, Ange. No one works on Australia

Day…Just come over for a bit. It would mean so much to your mother,' he replied. There was a beeping noise on Angela's phone.

'Look, I'm sorry Dad. I'm getting another call. I'll call you later, okay?' she said.

'Okay sweetheart. I love you.'

'I love you too, Dad.' She then pressed the button on her phone. The other call was connected. 'Hello?'

'It's me, Ken…The witness is prepared to come forward with the story.' Angela's eyes suddenly lit up.

'That's great, Ken…Is he going to testify?'

'Yes, he will. But he wants to meet with you first. Are you free?'

'Of course, I'd be happy to. But why does he want to meet with me now?' she asked, as she got up to get herself ready.

'He wants to make sure that you're credible.'

'Oh, come on, Ken. Surely, you'd put in a good word for me?' she replied, with sarcasm.

'This is serious, Angela. We're not messing around, and we're certainly not going to wait. We will go to another paper…I'm sure the Herald would love to get their hands on this.'

'No! Don't be stupid!' she said. 'I'm on my way now. Where shall I meet you?' she asked. She pressed the button on the elevator to go down.

'There's a parking garage a block from your office. Meet him there.'

'How will I know where he is?' asked Angela. There was a brief pause on the other end. The elevator doors opened, and Angela stepped in.

'He'll contact you once you get there,' said Ken. Suddenly, the call disconnected.

'But…hello?' Angela had no idea what she was getting into. Her heart was racing the whole time she rode the elevator.

Later, Angela made her way over to the parking garage. It was a multi-storey building and many of Angela's colleagues used the garage as it was close by and relatively cheap. She made her way into the building. It was quiet and there was the distant sound of tires screeching. As Angela wandered around in circles, waiting for the instructions, she tapped her shoe on the ground. She also took out her packet of cigarettes and lit one up. She was trying to quit smoking, but she struggled with it, and needed one desperately. She was stressed, which was not surprising. She stood there smoking her cigarette. Just then, her mobile phone started ringing. He looked at the screen and saw that it was an unknown number. She hesitated before answering it. 'Hello?'

'Is this Shaw?' a muffled voice answered.

'Yes. This is Angela Shaw,' she replied. There was another brief pause.

'Head to the third floor. Look for a silver Ford.' The call disconnected. At that, Angela headed the elevator. It took her up to the third floor. The elevator doors opened, and she stepped out. There were only about six or so vehicles parked on that level. She looked around. She spotted the silver Ford parked at the far end of the level. Her heart was racing even more now, and she had no idea what to expect. As she got closer to the car, one of the vehicle's doors opened. A man stepped out. He was wearing casual clothes and had a cap on his head. 'Are you Shaw?' asked the man. Angela slowly nodded.

'Yes. Angela Shaw, Capital Gazette. And you are?'

'A dead man walking,' he replied, as he looked around cautiously.

'It's okay, I wasn't followed…My contact said you're willing to come forward and testify against BMC. I need to know who you are?' she said. The man let out a sigh. 'Ron Kasper. I'm an Acquisitions Officer with BMC.'

'What is it that you know about the company that is so detrimental?' she asked. She got out her note pad in preparation to write.

'These guys are criminals. They've killed thousands of innocent people,' said Ron. 'In 2014, BMC were attempting to build a military operations bunker in East Timor. However, the land they were attempting to purchase was underneath a village. A village with over two thousand East Timorese,' said Ron. Angela was vigorously scribbling notes. She was also recording the conversation on her phone.

'So, what happened?'

'The villagers weren't happy about the plan. BMC tried to pay them to relocate, but they still wouldn't move. The land the village was on was sacred ground…So, BMC decided to take things to the next level…The entire village was murdered,' he explained.

Angela's eyes lit up. She couldn't believe what she was being told.

'Jesus Christ…You're saying that an Australian defence contractor authorized the execution of over two thousand innocent people of a foreign country?' she asked. Ron slowly nodded.

'Yes. They were determined to build the facility, as it would give them a strategic advantage. They covered up the genocide by stating it was a natural disaster.'

'I see…And what proof do you have that BMC were behind this?' she asked. This was the question she'd been waiting to get an answer.

'Because I acquired the weapons that were used in the massacre,' said Ron. 'I had no idea they were being used to commit genocide. I purchased the weapons on behalf of the company. That's what I do,' he said.

'I've got records of payments made by senior management and even records of the sign off of the weapons.'

'So, there's definitely a money trail…Where's this evidence now?'

'It's safe…It's on a disc drive in an encrypted folder.'

'Okay…If we're going to bring these people down, I need to know if you're willing to repeat this in court?' she asked. Ron didn't reply straight away. He looked around and then back at Angela.

'It has to be done properly. Once I go public with this information, I will become a target.'

'I know. I have friends in the AFP. They'll be

able to provide you with protection,' she said.

'Fine…Here's the evidence. Guard it with your life,' he said. He then passed over a thin black USB device. Angela took it. She held it in the palm of her hand and her heart dropped. Just then, Angela looked up as she saw a dark-coloured vehicle come speeding towards them. It all happened within a split second. The front passenger window was down, and the vehicle stopped. A gun shot was fired, followed by a second. Angela immediately dropped to the ground. She didn't know if she reacted first, but she felt a hand grabbing her on the way down. More shots were fired. Glass shattered. Angela couldn't do anything but lay there and scream for help. She covered her head as glass covered her. Finally, the shots finished, and then Angela heard the screeching sound of the car speeding off. Angela was in a complete state of shock. Her hands were trembling, and her heart raced a million miles an hour. 'Are you okay?' she quivered. She slowly looked up. There was blood and glass everywhere. Ron Kasper had been shot multiple times. 'Oh God.' Angela slowly crawled her entire body over to Ron. She pressed her fingers against his neck to check for a pulse. But there was none. Ron Kasper was dead. 'Shit!' she cursed.

She was in so much fright.

She couldn't move. It was as though her entire body was paralyzed. Finally, she found the courage to get to her feet. She felt her phone was vibrating and she quickly got it out to answer. 'Hello?' she said in a terrified voice.

'Hey, it's just me. What's wrong, are you okay?' it was Andrew Shaw, her husband. Angela took a moment to compose herself.

'No...I'm not okay. Something's happened...I need to see you right now!' she yelled.

'Jesus. Okay, ah. I'm still in town. I'll be home in twenty minutes,' he replied.

'Good. I'm in trouble. I need your help sweetheart. I'll speak to you soon,' she said, and then hung up. After she disconnected the call, she dialed triple zero. 'Yes, police. I need to report a shooting. A man has been shot. Get here as fast as you can!' she then hung up.

****

Sometime later, Angela returned to her apartment. She was still traumatized by what happened at the parking garage. It was approaching seven o'clock at night. No sign of her husband, Andrew. She was getting worried. She really needed to talk to him about all of this. She got out her smartphone to check for messages or calls, but there were none. Angela found herself sitting at the kitchen bench. She was sipping a glass of red wine. At the same time, she was going over some of the evidence she got from Ron Kasper. She managed to decrypt the file, and the evidence was highly disturbing. They were mostly images taken of dead bodies in East Timor, but there was also a short video. She watched it and was completely horrified by what was on it. This evidence was the key to bringing down Birchall McClelland. As she sipped her wine, she suddenly looked up to hear a loud noise. It sounded like a window shattering. Then she heard the distant sound of the neighbours' dogs barking. Angela put down the glass and got up to go and investigate the commotion. She looked in all the rooms. Finally, she went into the bathroom and saw that the window had been smashed by a brick. Probably some kids playing, she thought to herself. She relaxed a little bit, but she was still on edge. She then wandered back into the kitchen. The copy of the evidence she was making was complete. She'd also sent a digital copy of it to Andy, just as a precaution. All of a sudden, Angela was grabbed from behind. A hand pressed against her mouth. She went to scream but it was muffled by the glove. She began to struggle to break free. Her attacker pulled her from the bar stool, and it toppled over. She was thrown to the ground, and her head hit the large white tiles. Her skull cracked on impact. Blood began spilling out. Angela was still conscious, but she was in immense pain. She couldn't move, except gasp for air as she began to choke on her own blood. As she lay there, she kept alive long enough to see the shadowy figure of a man standing over her. He was wielding a gun. But he didn't kill her. He wanted to watch her slowly die. The man stood there. He hesitated for a moment, before taking out his mobile phone to dial a number. It rang multiple times before it answered. 'Yes?' a voice answered.

'Mr. Benedict, it's Mitch Clark.'

'Has the situation been taken care of?' Mitch Clark looked down at Angela Shaw. She was virtually dead.

'Yes, Sir. It's been dealt with. I'm just dealing with the cleanup.' As he waited for a response, he emptied a bottle of pills and scattered them all around Angela's body.

'Good. This needs to look like a suicide. We can't have anyone asking questions,' said the voice of Karl Benedict.

'Don't worry, Sir. I'm good at my job. There will be no evidence of my being here. The police will assume she overdosed. Case closed,' said Mitch.

'Excellent. Once you've done that, make sure her laptop is destroyed…You've done well, Agent Clark. Your payment will be transferred to your account within the hour.' A cheeky grin merged onto Mitch's face.

'Thank you, Mr. Benedict. I'll let you know when it's done.' He then hung up the phone and continued what he was doing.

Australia Day

2020

Mick Greer wasn't in the best of moods. He had been forced to do the one thing he'd never done to any of his detectives—Call them to work on their well-deserved day-off. Even though he knew that the detectives would understand, it still didn't help as he would have to face them all in a few minutes. This job was his life and the headquarters of the New South Wales Police Force in Sydney's Parramatta, his home. Mick was the Detective Senior Sergeant and in charge of the Organised Crime Squad. His superior was Anna Mackenzie, the Chief

Inspector. She was, in his words, a hard ass. She was career-focused and didn't have much time for workplace drama. As his mind spun with the dilemma he was in, the elevator dinged and slid open, allowing him to step off and walk across the main floor to a not so happy place. He approached a door with the nameplate; Anna Mackenzie and below was her title, Chief Inspector. He took a deep breath and knocked. He waited for a response before opening the door. He stepped in and saw that Anna was talking on the phone, probably to her superior. 'Yes, I can assure you Sir, we'll take care of it,' she said and then hung up. 'Ah Mick do come in,' she said, turning her attention to him.

'Morning, Chief Inspector. I was told this was an urgent situation?' Anna nodded and took a sip of her coffee.

'Yes, it is. We've had a priority situation called in from the AFP. They wanted us to deal with it,' she said.

'And what exactly is it?' Anna didn't reply straight away. She knew Mick was pissed.

'I will brief you and the team directly, but suffice it to say, there's been an assassination threat against the President of Australia,' she said. The room fell silent after that, and Mick's eyes widened.

'Shit. Do we know who's involved?'

'Like I said, I'll brief you fully with the other detectives. Are they here yet?' Mick nodded.

'Yes. Detectives Cooper and Faulkner are here,' he responded.

'Good. What's happening at the Opera House?' Since today was all about the Republic of Australia's birth, the New South Wales Police Force was tasked with providing security for the President's arrival, as was the AFP.

'We've got additional officers on-site and security sweeps have been completed,' said Mick. 'I've also got Felicity running surveillance drones over the site.'

'Perfect. It's time to go brief the team. Let's go,' said Anna, as she stood up. She took one last sip of her coffee before slipping on her blazer. What was needed now was efficiency and speed. Together, Anna and Mick made a brisk walk across the floor, bypassing offices, and personnel before approaching the briefing room. Being a gentleman and despite not liking Anna that much, he opened the glass door for her, allowing her to go in first. It was a large corner room with two sides as windows that had a great view of the city. Mick followed Anna into the room and slipped onto one of the chairs. There were about a dozen or so detectives and officers in the room. In the front were Detectives Ethan Cooper and Diane Faulkner. Felicity Meyers, a Technical Specialist, was in a seat next to Mick Greer, operating a laptop and her fingers ready to take notes.

'Morning, all...' Anna started. 'I apologise

for making you come in today. But, as you know, today is an important day for this country, so we have to act accordingly and make sure everything goes smoothly,' she said. 'We have a serious situation on our hands…The AFP has identified a threat to the Australia Day festival.. In particular, they've identified an assassination threat to the President's life,' she explained. The room fell silent after that as everyone had a look of shock on their faces.

'Bloody hell,' Detective Senior Constable Ethan Cooper cursed.

'Surely we've been getting threats ever since they announced the republic?' Detective Senior Constable Diane Faulkner asked.

'That's true, but the AFP and ASIO has confirmed the validity of the threat. They suspect the terrorists involved are highly sophisticated and deeply connected within the AFP and security,' she explained.

'Do we know who is behind the threat?'

asked Mick, looking directly at Anna. She gave him a look.

'The AFP suspects the threat is being funded and managed by crime boss Karl Benedict,' she said. 'Benedict continues to evade us, but we've determined he's the one we need to focus our attention to,' she said. 'Benedict has a large network of personnel at his disposal. We need to devote all our resources into finding him,' she added. 'This threat is real. Which is why the Commissioner has increased security for the President, who is expected to arrive here in Sydney within the hour,' she said. 'So, I need all departments working on this. No lead should go ignored. This is one of the most historic days for Australia, and if something should happen, the integrity of this nation will be destroyed.' Again, no one said anything. 'Alright, let's get to work. I want updates every fifteen minutes.' Anna went back to her paperwork, while everyone started making their way out of the meeting room. As he left Felicity Meyers came over to him.

'Excuse me Boss, there's someone here to see you,' she said.

'Who is it?' he asked.

'He says his name is Shane Murphy. He said you know him?' she said. Mick's eyes widened at that.

'You did say Murphy right?' she slowly nodded.

'Yeah, who is he?'

'Someone I know. Where is he?'

'I sent him into your office. Is that okay?'

'It's fine, thanks.' He was very curious as to why Shane was here. He took a sip of his coffee and headed over to his office. He opened the door and sitting in his chair was Shane Murphy.

'Detective Greer, nice office,' he said. There was a sudden pause.

'What the bloody hell are you doing here?' he snapped.

As she stared at her reflection in the vanity she was leaning against, Charmaine Bradley could feel the Boeing 787 jet she was flying on, dip slightly. Just so slightly, that she wondered if it had been her imagination. This was only her second time using the Air Force jet that was exclusively for her use as the President of Australia, and she knew she wouldn't be getting used to travelling in style for a little while longer. Charmaine was the first President in Australian history after the country cut ties with the British Commonwealth a year ago and became a republic. Charmaine, the President of the Republic of Australia and the first woman to be one too, was elected six months ago. She had taken over from the Governor-General and was on her way to give her first speech since being sworn in. It was Australia Day today, and it had been publicised nationwide that the new President would be giving her maiden address at the Sydney Opera House. A major festival had been organised in conjunction with the birth of the republic. As she held on to the countertop to observe herself, Charmaine muttered a few words softly, 'You've got this, Charmaine. You can do it. You've come this far... So, this is just another small step.' She knew she had loads of work cut out for her, and she was ready to do it. It was just that she couldn't help but feel quite small now, as compared to the entity that was Australia. It was going to be hard work. She took one last look at her beautiful blonde face before walking out of the bathroom to her office aboard the jet.

This was the Australian equivalent of Air Force One, the designated name of any plane that carried on board the President of the United States. It was brand new, only bought and commissioned a month ago to prepare for the transition of government to that of a republic. When she got to her office, the two Protective Security Officers escorting her stopped and took their positions on either side of the door. They were dressed in black suits and equipped with earpiece microphones to communicate with command on the ground.

'Good morning, Madam President.' A warm and husky voice greeted her. Joseph Parsons, the President's Official Secretary who also happened to be a good family friend of over twenty years, stepped up from where he stood waiting with a warm smile. She picked him mainly for the fact that she trusted his cool and wise head. They had also worked together for over two decades and this was another reason she had insisted on giving him the appointment. Joe's job responsibilities included providing the President with all the necessary support she needed to carry out her constitutional, ceremonial, and public duties, as well as assist with administrative tasks and organise her schedule each week. She flashed him a warm smile back and went to sit at her desk. Once she was seated, Joe approached the table with a concerned look and asked, 'How are you doing today?' Charmaine grinned conspiratorially, 'I'm scared as hell, Joe.' There was a slight pause, after which they both shared a laugh.

'I understand. It can be daunting.' He smiled at her as he passed her a report.

'You know it. Let's watch the news while I go through this.' Joe turned on the TV and tuned in to a station that showed a reporter at the Opera House chattering excitedly at the camera. She showed how exciting the dozens of enthusiastic supporters behind her found Australia Day. The crowd was gradually being stoked as they celebrated and at the same time, waited to see their President. The number of blue fields with little Union Jacks behind her went as far as the eye could see. Charmaine sat there in her chair, staring at the TV, and sunk into a distant memory. She thought about the night she was appointed President. It was supposed to be a celebratory evening but went horribly wrong.

'...And welcome back from the break, I'm your host Tony Wyatt. Now, we've come to the moment you've all been waiting for. I'd like to bring out tonight's special guest...She has been dubbed 'The Australian'...Ladies and gentlemen, please welcome the Australian Head of State and the first female president, ...Charmaine Bradley!' The audience stood up and started clapping and cheering with excitement. Some even whistled, as Charmaine

Bradley stepped out onto the stage. She had a big smile on her face and waved at everyone as she approached the desk. The TV host, Tony Wyatt stood up and shook her hand. They briefly exchanged words, but no one could hear what they were saying because of the noise from the audience. 'Madam President, welcome, welcome!' said Tony, as they sat down again. 'Welcome to the show.'

'Thank you, it's great to be here!' said Charmaine, as she got herself comfortable. The audience clapped again.

'So…Madam President…That is weird saying that, huh?'

'You're telling me! I'm still not used to it,' she said, with a laugh.

'Of course, of course…Now, I'd like to be the first to say, congratulations on the appointment,' he said. Everyone started clapping again.

'Thank you, still not used to that either.'

'How are you feeling?'

'Oh, wow. You know, overwhelmed is probably how I'd describe it,' she said.

'Yeah, I bet.'

'It's hard to believe that something like this has actually happened in this country,' said Charmaine.

'Now, I know most of the audience knows about the position of the president, but can you tell us a little bit about what you'll be doing?'

'Definitely, I mean, for the most part, it'll be basically what the Governor-General does. Official appointments of government ministers, dissolving parliament, etc, and a lot of it will be going to functions and events and giving back to you guys who got me here,' she said, pointing to the audience, who in turn, cheered and clapped.

'Wow, that's great! And so tell us, what's happening on Australia Day?'

'Yes, that's a big one. As you know it will be

the 200th Anniversary of the arrival of the British, so it was such a great honour to be able to deliver my maiden speech as Australia's first president,' she said. 'Also, I'll be officially signing Australia's new Constitution as a republic.' More cheers and whistles could be heard. 'And you know, it's just such a fantastic opportunity to be chosen to serve as Australia's first official head of state...' just then, she was interrupted when a member of the audience was shouting. 'Oi!' he said. Everyone focused their attention on him, confused as to what was going on. 'Oi! Do you know what this has done to our bloody country?' he shouted. The man was making his way down the steps towards the main stage. 'It's people like you who are going to destroy this country! People are gonna hate you for it!'

'Sir, I'm not quite sure what you're referring to, but I can assure you that this change to become a republic will benefit Australians,' she said, but she was abruptly cut off.

'That's bloody bull shit!' the man shouted. He was still charging down the steps. 'This country is not ready to be a republic. You know it, and I know it! You're gonna bring this country to its knees!'

'Can we get security in here?' said Tony, as he stood up, removing his microphone piece. Security personnel started coming in hot. 'I'm not gonna let that happen! Go die you bloody bitch!' he shouted. At that, the man reached into his jacket pocket and pulled out a handgun. 'Gun!' a security officer shouted. Another leapt at Charmaine, who was already on her feet. The man fired a shot. People started screaming and fumbling all over each other. More shots could be heard.

John and Charmaine Bradley had been together for the past twenty-odd years and loved each other very much. Since his wife, Charmaine entered a life of politics, John had supported her every single day and wanted her to be successful. After his wife was appointed the first President of Australia, John became the First Gentleman of Australia and was a well-liked man. However, he had been suffering from depression, as well as grief. Six months ago, he and Charmaine lost their daughter, Angela Shaw. She allegedly committed suicide, but it was never confirmed. For the past six months, her death had been in the papers, and it was a daily hot topic for news channels. After a thorough investigation by the Australian Federal Police, it was revealed that she did in fact commit suicide, and the case was closed. But of course, John refused to believe it. He was convinced that her death was not a suicide, and that someone had murdered her. He spent the last couple of weeks attempting to find out the truth about her death. Charmaine knew John was struggling with her death, and they agreed that he should seek help from a professional. John was in Canberra still, while Charmaine made her way to Sydney. John Bradley sat staring at the woman in front of him who was just scheduling their next appointment. Being the First Gentleman of Australia, it was becoming increasingly hard to get anywhere without being recognised and the media surrounding the place. They were that much of a sensation. And that was if he went with his protective escort. On days like these when he went out with only one, he had to try his best to blend in with the public and thankfully, no one had discovered that the husband to the President came here to meet with his shrink every week. John just couldn't get over the death of Angela. It had been six months since Angela Shaw was found lying lifeless in her apartment, but every time he thought about it, it seemed like a fresh wound that had happened just the day before. He couldn't get over the grief, and the fact that the police had ruled out foul play was difficult to accept. He knew her daughter, knew her more than anyone on this earth did, and he knew Angela couldn't have killed herself. She just couldn't. She had a beautiful mind, and she had been happy. Very happy. There was no way Angela could've been depressed. She loved her job as an investigative journalist simply because it was fun and exciting for her. Just then, John's bodyguard,

Mitch Clark, came in. 'Excuse me, Mr. Bradley. You have a phone call,' he said, holding a phone.

'Excuse me, we're not quite done here,' said Emily, his psychologist.

'It's okay, Emily...I could use a break anyway,' said John. He came over to Mitch, who stood by the door. 'Who is it?' he asked. Mitch leaned forward.

'It's Derek Miller, Sir,' said Mitch. John's eyes widened with excitement. He took the phone and walked away from Mitch.

'Derek, it's John,' he answered curtly. 'You have something?'

'Hi John, sorry to bother you. As a matter of fact, I may have come across some new evidence. I'd like to meet in person and discuss if you don't mind.'

'Not at all. Let's meet at the agreed place. I'll be there right away,' John was already half out of his seat. He hung up and looked at his psychologist, asking her to place a call about the new appointment before leaving the office with his bodyguard in tow. This was one of the results of countless nights and days worrying over what had happened to Angela. Less than three weeks ago, he had decided to take things into his own hands by hiring a Private Investigator. Now, it seemed like it was paying off.

'What's happening, Sir?' asked Mitch Clark, his bodyguard. They were making their way out of the office.

'Derek has some more information about Angela. I need you to take me to the meeting location,' he said.

'Again?' Mitch had been against the idea of hiring a Private Investigator, as he feared he was exploiting him. 'Sir, we're due to be in Sydney in the next hour.' Mitch checked his watch.

'Please, Mitch. I have to do this first. I can

take full responsibility if you get any slack from your superiors,' said John. Mitch just stood there and let out a sigh.

'Fine. Let's go.' John smiled at that. Mitch went over and opened the back door to John's escort vehicle, a sleek, black Range Rover Sports edition. One of the many perks of being a VIP was having his own private transport and security. Mitch knew he was doing the wrong thing, but it was his job to protect John and not question his decisions. After all, without him, he wouldn't have a job.

****

It was a short flight from Canberra – 50 minutes to be exact – the Australian Air Force Boeing 787 Dreamliner VIP jet touched down at Sydney's Kingsford Smith Airport. The jet was sleek and shiny and painted with the Australian Air Force colour scheme on its fuselage. It also had the words: REPUBLIC OF AUSTRALIA, written on either side. It taxied to the general aviation section of the airport where a group of people were waiting there to meet the President of Australia. It finally came to a stop and the plane was surrounded by ground service personnel. A vehicle was parked there waiting for the president. It was a black Range Rover Sports with tinted windows. When the plane stopped its cabin door opened. A few moments later, Charmaine Bradley emerged from inside the plane. Reporters, photographers, civilians, and security were waiting anxiously as the light blue Dreamliner VIP jet with white stars and gold leaves came to a halt in front of them. The crowds erupted in cheers and the clicking of the cameras roar to life when Charmaine Bradley stepped out from the jet flanked by Joe Parsons, security, and several of her staff. She made her way down to the crowd on the way to the black cars waiting for her. Along the way she posed for pictures, hugged children, and greeted several members. As she got nearer to the cars, Kevin Fraser, the Premier of New South Wales emerged from one with an abnormally large smile on his face that shows off all of his teeth. 'Madam President, this is Kevin Fraser, the Premier of New South Wales,' said Joe.

'Madam President, it is a pleasure to finally meet you,' he said, as they shook hands.

'Thank you, Premier. I'm excited to be here. It's going to be a great day for the festival,' she said. They both stood there and smiled at the photographers for a few moments.

'Ma'am, we need to get moving,' said Joe.

'Very well. Thank you for coming, Premier. I'll see you at the Opera House,' she said. She and Joe walked over to the vehicle. They climbed into the back and it slowly drove away. The whole time, photographers were snapping photos of the President. 'Thanks for the save, Joe,' she added.

'No problem, Ma'am. Happy to help any time.'

After a quick twenty-minute drive from the airport, the President's vehicle finally arrived the Admiralty House in Kirribilli. The Admiralty House was in the suburb of Kirribilli, on the northern foreshore of Sydney Harbour. It sat adjacent to Kirribilli House, the official residence of the Prime Minister of Australia. It was a large Victorian Regency and Italianate sandstone manor with lush greenery surrounding the residence and occupies the tip of Kirribilli Point. It boasted striking views of the city with the Sydney Harbour Bridge and the Sydney Opera House to the right. A large iron gate with spiked tops secured the main entrance and a security outbuilding patrolled by a security officer controlled who gained access to the residence and when. The cast iron gates opened inward and moments later, the black Range Rover Sports slowly pulled in. It was carrying the first President of Australia, Charmaine Bradley. The vehicle drove down the gravel driveway and came to a stop at the main entrance. The car sat there for a moment, and Charmaine was reluctant to get out. She sat there and could see there was a group of reporters and photographers standing nearby the main entrance to the Admiralty House. They were all clicking away, taking photos of the President's car. Joe sat in the seat next to her, and he knew that she was distressed. 'Ma'am, everything okay?' he asked, as he gently pressed his hand on her shoulder. Charmaine smiled.

'I'll be okay, thanks Joe. Just trying to come

to terms with all of this. It's certainly overwhelming,' she replied. Joe nodded.

'I can understand that. But it will get easier, trust me,' said Joe. She thought for a moment, before responding.

'I hope so.' She took a deep breath and was preparing herself. At that, Charmaine stepped out. She was immediately bombarded by the reporters, all chanting questions at her. She was literally blinded by the flicker of flashes from the photographers' cameras. She was greeted by each state's Governor, who were planning to sign the new Constitution under the republic system. Charmaine smiled as she approached them and began shaking hands, one by one. The photographers were taking photos of the President shaking hands with the Governors. The whole meet and greet took about five minutes. After which, the state Governors and Charmaine Bradley made their way into the residence. They were escorted down the corridor and ventured into the lounge room where the signing was to take place. But before Charmaine went to enter the room, she was stopped by Joe who had been on the phone. 'Ma'am, sorry to interrupt. I've received a call from the Police Force. Chief Inspector Anna Mackenzie would like a word,' he said. Charmaine looked at him, oddly.

'What's this about, Joe?' she asked.

'I'm not sure, Ma'am. But she said it was urgent.' Charmaine didn't reply straight away and looked back at the lounge room where the Governors were conversing.

'Okay, Joe. I'll take the call,' she replied, and Joe handed her the phone. She walked away a few metres to talk privately. 'This is the President.'

'Madam President, I'm Anna Mackenzie, Chief Inspector of the Organised Crime Squad.'

'Yes, Ms. Mackenzie. I was told this was an urgent matter?'

'It is, Ma'am. I'm calling to inform you that my agency has identified that there is the possibility of a threat to your life, which is supposed to take place today,' she explained.

'My God…Who's responsible for this threat?' she asked.

'We're not a hundred percent sure on that, Ma'am. But we do know it is a credible threat,' she said. Charmaine let out a sigh. 'Ma'am, I'm calling because I believe that you should strongly consider postponing the Australia Day festival,' said Anna.

'No, absolutely not. Chief Inspector today is an historical event. The entire country is watching the event on live television. If we postpone the festival, it will ruin the whole thing,' said Charmaine.

'I realise that, Ma'am. But we're talking about a terrorist threat. Dozens, if not hundreds of lives are at stake, not to mention yours,' said Anna.

'Listen, Ms. Mackenzie…I'm about to sign the most important document in Australian history. Then, I will be going on live TV to give my inaugural speech as President…You have until 12PM to neutralise this terrorist threat,' said Charmaine.

'That doesn't give us much time, Ma'am.'

'Then I'd suggest you get to work, Ms. Mackenzie,' said Charmaine. There was a brief pause.

'Yes, thank you, Madam President.' Then Charmaine hung up the call. She walked over to Joe, who was standing by the door.

'The Police want to postpone the festival.' Joe's eyes widened.

'What for?'

'They said there's been a threat to my life. I told them they have until 12PM to stop the terrorists,' she said. 'Keep me updated on the situation, Joe.' He slowly nodded. As Charmaine handed him the phone back, she went inside the main lounge room. Inside, the Governors were standing around, waiting patiently. 'Gentlemen, ladies. I appreciate you all waiting...I'd like to get started with the signing,' she said.

****

For the past ten minutes, Mick Greer and Shane Murphy had been talking. Mostly about what Shane had been doing with himself lately and how his family had been. Mick hadn't seen Shane for a good couple of years, he'd just up and disappeared out of nowhere. 'Sorry to trouble you at work, but this couldn't wait, buddy,' said Shane.

'What's going on, Shane? You disappear for two years, then all of a sudden you show up in my office,' he said. Shane didn't reply straight away and looked around.

'I came to find out what you know about this

investigation,' he said, changing the subject.

'I know that someone is planning to attack the Australia Day festival,' said Mick.

'Yes, and I know who's behind the attack.' Mick's eyes widened. He slowly sat down on the chair.

'And who exactly is that?' asked Mick.

'Karl Benedict...Well, someone who works for Karl Benedict, but his company is definitely involved,' said Shane. Mick's eyes widened.

'Yeah, my team just got briefed on the situation. They suspect Benedict is involved but don't actually have any proof,' he said. 'So BMC is involved?' Shane slowly nodded.

'Yes, they are...I've been working as a mercenary for him these past two years to see if I could get close to Benedict. His company is corrupt and power hungry. But they're also against the idea of this nation becoming a republic,' he explained. 'Now that we've severed ties with the British, it's going to be a lot harder for companies like BMC to get away with stuff without heavy repercussions,' he said.

'I see. And what makes you think BMC is involved with the terror plot?'

'Benedict has highly trained mercenaries at his disposal. He also has access to weapons and explosives,' he said.

'Shit. Then we'd better start work on finding out who else is involved at BMC.' He reached over to pick up the phone.

'Felicity Meyers.'

'Felicity, I need you to pull up all financial and employment records of Birchall McClelland,' he requested.

'Yes, Sir. I'll get on it.' He then turned back to Shane.

'There's something else you need to know. I found out who the go-to guy is for Benedict's weapons and explosives unit.'

'Who is it?'

'Mark Hauser. If anyone knows what these guys are planning, it's him,' he said.

'Fantastic. Where's this Mark Hauser character live?'

'He's in Balmain. I've got an address, but I wanted to let you know before I went to pay him a visit,' said Shane. Mick thought for a moment.

'Are you sure this information is legitimate?' he asked, as he stood up to put on his blazer.

'Of course, Mick. You know me, I'd never give you false information. Plus, I don't want anything bad to happen today. It's too important,' he said. Mick hesitated before replying.

'Alright, let's go chat to this guy.'

John couldn't get over what Derek Miller told him. The fact that Angela's husband, Andrew Shaw received a considerable sum of money two days after her suicide raised some concerning questions. He was going to get to the bottom of this no matter what. He was on his way over to Andrew's apartment, as he knew where he lived. He was nervous about the whole thing. It would be a lie to say he wasn't. This was the first time he would be seeing Andrew since his daughter's funeral, but he just had no choice. He had to find out what the money Andrew had gotten was for, and if it was related to Angela's death. As the car pulled up at the suburban residence that was their destination, Mitch Clark, John's personal bodyguard of six months, couldn't help but look back over his shoulder to ask his boss from the steering wheel. 'Is this a good idea, Sir?' There was concern in his voice. But John's mind was made up, and there was steel in his voice when he replied,

'I don't know if this is the right thing to do, but I have to find out what Andrew knows.' Mitch nodded and parked the car, before coming down to hold it open for the First Gentleman of the country. John knocked on the door to his son in-law's house again. It used to be his daughter's house too, he thought to himself in despair. Angela's house was located in Yarralumla, a suburb of Canberra. Perhaps the man wasn't home, he mused and decided to leave. But then he heard noises at the door, just a few seconds before the door opened to reveal the man who had been married to his daughter not so long ago. Andrew's face was nothing exceptional, in fact it was the glasses he wore to help his short-sighted vision that made his appearance a bit more remarkable. He was wearing a shirt that looked like he hadn't taken it off in days and the stubble on his jaw showed that he hadn't shaved for as long, either. He was surprised to see the First Gentleman on his doorstep. 'John! W-what are y-you doing here?' he stuttered.

'Hi Andy, long time no speak,' said John, in a serious tone.

'Likewise,…Come on in, come in,' Andrew said, stammering a bit in surprise. He opened the door for the two of them to step in and closed it behind them. Still talking, he followed behind to usher them into seats. 'If I had known you were coming, I would have gotten something prepared. Would you like a drink, maybe a beer?' John shook his head slightly, preparing himself to say,

'I'm sorry Andrew, but I won't be staying long. I've got a plane to catch shortly. I'm heading to Sydney for the festival.'

'I see. Pretty exciting, I bet. I'm so pleased for Ms. Bradley,' he said. Andrew was in the kitchen busy making a coffee.

'Look, this isn't really a social visit.'

'I d-don't understand. What do you mean by that?'

'I've come to ask you what you know about my daughter's death. Is there something you know about Angela's death that you don't want others to know?' John finally let it out. There was an awkward silence in the room. 'I'm sorry. I d-don't understand what you mean by that. What are you trying to say, John?' Andrew asked, looking confused.

'Okay. Let me put it this way. You received a

rather large amount of money just three days after Angela died. Would you like to tell me what that was about?' John probed, looking into the younger man's bloodshot eyes.

'I still don't know what you're talking about, John. What's the meaning of this? What exactly are you trying to say?'

'Stop lying, Andy. How do you think I know about the money? What was the money for?' he demanded.

'That's my business, John! I don't see any reason for you to be bringing that up.'

'Wrong! It's my business because it's too close to my daughter's death for me not to feel uncomfortable! Now tell me. What was the money for?' he snapped, getting red in the face from anger. Andrew sighed, placing his head in his hands. Since it had come to this, there really wasn't any need for him to lie about it.

'Yes, I got some money. It's an Inheritance. My father just died recently you know that right?' he said, somberly. 'I just got what he left to me.'

'I don't think so. I don't think so at all. That's not it, I'm sure. It can't be that simple!' John insisted, raising his voice.

'You need to calm down, John! You can as well find out if I'm lying or not. Now... If not for the respect I have towards you and your wife, I would have asked you to leave this house the moment you implied that I had something to do with my wife's death...She was my wife you know! My wife!'

Faced with the outburst of the recently bereaved widower, John finally realized how insensitive and inconsiderate he had been in his grief driven mission to find out what had happened to Angela.

'I'm sorry, Andrew. I didn't realize how inconsiderate I was being...I'm really sorry,' he apologized, repeatedly.

'You can confirm the truth of what I said. I'm

sure you have your sources. Now if you'll permit me, I haven't been able to stop mourning my wife, and I would like to be alone for now,' said Andrew, his voice a bit cold.

****

Inside the black SUV that was John's vehicle, the man sat with wracked nerves at the thought of what had happened with Andrew. John could not believe how completely insensitive he had been with his son in-law. The truth was that even now, John wasn't sure whether to believe if the money was truly an Inheritance or was for something else. Andrew's father had been dead for more than three months. 'To the airport, Sir?' Mitch asked from behind the wheel, jarring him back to reality.

'Yes, yes. I need to be with my wife as soon as possible.' Mitch nodded and focused back on the road, just as John's phone rang out in the enclosed space.

'Hello, darling.' It was his wife. Charmaine's hurried voice came over the phone.

'John. How are you, and where are you? You're supposed to be here.' It was obvious she was rushing to make the call and wanted to check up on him.

'I'm okay. I'm heading over to you now. I was just err, I was just at Andrew's,' John confessed.

'What? Why did you go visit him? Is something wrong with him?' She asked, curiously.

'Nothing, really. I, I just...' The man was at a loss for what to say.

'I don't get it. Is something the matter, John? Why did you go see Andrew?'

'Well, see thing is...I uhm, I recently hired an investigator to help with finding out what happened with, with Angela and I-'

'You bloody did what?' Charmaine

interrupted as her voice went a few octaves higher. 'You did what, John?'

'I hired an investigator, and he found something, so I, I had to go see Andrew to clear up a few things. That's all.'

'John, I don't get it! The police said it was suicide, and the coroner's report didn't say otherwise. How can you insist on your wild goose hunt by making a mountain out of nothing when you know very clearly how much you're hurting all of us?' Charmaine demanded, her voice heating up in her upset. John didn't back down then. He never did.

'But I know she didn't kill herself! We both know that darling. Angela was happier more than anything in the last year after they got married! You of all people should know this, so don't you want to support me and find out what went wrong too!'

'No. It's not that I don't want to support you. It's that you're just making everyone suffer in your needless obsession, John. And it's affecting all of us.'

'That's not it! I'd like to know how you can be this faithless in our daughter. I wonder how!'

'You know what John? I have to go now. I have to go to the Opera House to give my speech,' she said, fighting back the tears. 'Maybe we'll talk about this once the event is over?'

'Fine.' John just hung up, abruptly.

About five minutes later, John Bradley's vehicle arrived at Canberra Airport. Sitting on the tarmac was an Australian Air Force Dassault Falcon 7X VIP jet. It was a twin-engine special purpose aircraft catering specifically for the First Gentleman of Australia. John's vehicle pulled up nearby the jet. Its engines were revving up and the crew were preparing it for takeoff. John was sitting in the back seat of his car, still feeling defeated by the fact that Charmaine had dismissed his help to solve the mystery behind Angela's death. But perhaps she was right. Maybe he needed to take a step back and accept the fact that Angela killed herself? Mitch parked the car. He got out and opened the door for John. Still feeling sorry for himself, he picked himself up and started making his way across the tarmac to the plane's exterior stairs. As he boarded the plane, he reached into his pocket in a daze to bring out his phone and take the call that was coming through. He suspected it was Charmaine again, but it wasn't. 'John Bradley,' he answered in a loud voice. It was quite noisy due to the turbine engines starting up.

'Hello?'

'Hey, John? It's Andrew,' said the quiet voice on the other end.

'W-what? Andrew what are you-- Look, I'm sorry, okay.' He started to apologise again. He was certainly surprised to be hearing from Andy again after what happened this morning.

'Are you still in Canberra?' he asked. John was already on the plane, but they hadn't moved yet, thankfully.

'Ah, yes. Just. I'm just about to takeoff though. What's wrong, Andy?' he asked. There was a pause.

'Look, I can't talk about this over the phone. Can you meet me somewhere? I'll text the address.' Andrew asked furtively. John didn't know how to respond at first.

'Oh. I don't know. I... Okay text it to me. I'll come now.' As John hung up, his head couldn't stop ringing and the first thing he thought of, was how Charmaine was going to be sorry she hadn't believed him. He was sure of it. Now, he just had to convince Mitch to drive him back to the city. Mitch climbed the stairs and boarded the plane, carrying the First Gentleman's bags. 'Mitch. Sorry to do this, but I have to go back to the city.' Mitch dropped the bags in frustration.

'But Sir, I have to get you to Sydney in the next hour. The President...'

'Will be fine without me. Please, Mitch. I

need to see this through. Andy just contacted me and wanted to meet with me. It has to do with Angela's death,' he explained. He could see that Mitch was frustrated. 'Please, Mitch. Do this for me. I promise, this is the last time.' Mitch hesitated before responding.

'Okay, fine. Let's go.'

****

Discussions of the new Constitution of the Republic of Australia were finally coming to an end. For the past fifteen minutes or so, Charmaine Bradley had been listening to each Governor speak and voice their opinions about the new system and how it all works. Of course, they'd already had numerous discussions after the referendum went through, but this was to be the final discussion before the Constitution was signed. Charmaine Bradley stood and interrupted the Governor of Queensland who was having a heated debate with the Governor of Victoria. There was much debate about the leadership roles and responsibilities by each of the state's Governors. 'Ladies and gentlemen, I apologize for the interruption, but we are on a tight schedule. We need to head over to the Opera House for the Independence Day festival. I'd like to take this opportunity to thank you all for your continued support in this transition phase,' said Charmaine. At that, the Governors stood up and started clapping. Then, Joe Parsons came in and he was holding a large A3 sheet of paper. It contained the Constitution of the Republic of Australia. At the bottom of the page was a space for the signatures of each state Governor, and of course, the President of Australia. The Governor of Queensland was the first to sign. As he did so, several photographers took photos of him affixing his name and signature. He shook hands with the President. Next to sign, was the Governor of

New South Wales. He scribbled his signature on the document and shook hands with the President. The Governor of Victoria was next in line to sign the document. He was then followed by the Governor of Tasmania. After the Governor of Tasmania, the Governor of South Australia signed the Constitution. Next up was the Governor of Western Australia, who was then followed by the Administrator of the Northern Territory. The last person to sign the Constitution was of course, the President of the Republic of Australia, Charmaine Bradley. After she scribbled her signature on the document, the Governors applauded, and more photos were taken. Standing nearby, Joe Parsons was watching as Charmaine shook hands with each Governor. Just then, Joe's mobile phone started ringing. It was on vibrate so as to not disturb this important moment. He then slipped away unnoticed to take the call.

'Joe Parsons.'

'Mr. Parsons, this is Anna Mackenzie, Chief Inspector of the Organised Crime Squad, New South Wales Police,' she said.

'What can I do for you, Chief Inspector?' asked Joe, looking confused.

'Sir, I'm calling because we have a situation. Our agency is currently investigating a potential threat to the President,' she explained.

'Bloody hell. Are you sure about this?'

'Yes, Sir. The AFP has confirmed the threat. They suspect someone is plotting to assassinate the President.'

'My God…Well, what's being done about this?' Joe looked back at the President as he saw her talking with the Governors.

'We are conducting a thorough investigation, Sir. But at the moment, we're unsure if we'll be able to stop this threat.'

'Well, that's unacceptable, Mackenzie.'

'I know, but what I'm suggesting is that the President postpone her attendance at the festival,' Mick suggested.

'Absolutely not, Chief Inspector. If the President doesn't arrive at the Opera House at 12pm as scheduled, she will become a laughingstock,' said Joe.

'It would be better than her being dead,' she replied. There was a pause.

'Look, this is the most important day for this nation. Everything is arranged for us to be there by lunch time. We can't afford any delays. Just fix this problem, Chief Inspector!' said Joe, abruptly. Then he hung up. He looked up from the phone and saw the President talking with several Governors. He was now worried about the President's safety.

Detective Senior Sergeant Mick Greer and Shane Murphy finally arrived in Balmain, a suburb of Sydney. They pulled up a few hundred metres away from Ennis Street so they were not detected by the suspect. Mick and Shane got out of the car. Together, they sprinted down the footpath, in a flanked position. Shane was behind Mick and covered his back. They got to Ennis Street and slowly made their way down it. Mick and Shane approached the front gate to the townhouse. It looked like no one was home, but they had to check it out regardless. Shane carefully lifted the latch on the gate so it didn't make any noise. He pushed it forward just enough for them to get through. Then they slowly made their way up the concrete footpath. Ever so cautiously, the two stepped onto the front veranda. Shane nodded at Mick and he opened the fly-screen door. He went to knock, but the door pushed open as soon as he touched it. Mick was suspicious by this and immediately withdrew his Glock 22 handgun, a standard weapon of choice for detectives of the Organised Crime Squad. Slowly, Mick stepped into the house. The house was run down and by the looks of things, someone had trashed the place. There was pieces of paper scattered everywhere and furniture smashed to bits. 'Hello!' Mick called out. 'This is Detective Senior Sergeant Mick Greer, with the Organised Crime Squad. New South Wales Police Force!'

There was no response. Mick started walking down the corridor, taking one step at a time. His gun raised in front of him, ready. They slowly made their way down the corridor. Just then, Mark Hauser stepped out with a shotgun in his hands.

'Get the fuck out of my house!' he shouted. His hands were shaking as he aimed the shotgun at Mick and Shane.

'Take it easy. We just want to ask you a few questions,' said Mick. He thought for a moment, then slowly lowered his gun.

'Mick, what are you doing?' asked Shane, confused by his move.

'Come on, think about it. If you pull that trigger, you're going to jail for the rest of your life,' said Mick. 'Please, we just want to ask you some questions.' Finally, Mick's words seemed to be helping. Mark slowly lowered his shotgun. At that, Shane moved in and slammed Mark against the wall. 'Murphy take it easy!'

Mick shouted.

'This guy is a thug, Mick. We can't go easy on him,' said Shane.

'He's our only connection to the terrorist threat,' said Mick. He walked up to Mark. 'Tell us what you know about the terrorist attack on the Australia Day festival. How is it being carried out?' he demanded. But of course, Mark didn't say anything. Shane had him in an arm lock and pushed him into the wall to get him to talk.

'I swear, I don't know anything.'

'I don't believe you. We know Karl Benedict hired you to take possession of a weapon, now tell us what the plan is!' Shane demanded, still pushing him into the wall. He was also gripping his hand tighter, making him whelp in pain. 'Tell me what the plan is!' Shane started bending his fingers back. Mark whelped again. Mick was standing there watching, not looking impressed by what he was doing.

'Okay! Okay! I'll tell you!' he shouted, trying not to burst into tears from the pain.

'Who else is involved?' Shane yelled.

'Okay…His name…is…Gregory Hughes,' he said, in deep breaths. He was in a lot of pain. 'I don't know where he is now…But Karl Benedict hired him to take out the President,' he explained. Shane looked at Mick who was in a bit of shock.

'Son of a bitch,' Mick said. He then immediately took out his mobile to dial a number.

'Anna Mackenzie,' Anna answered.

'Boss, I just searched a property in Balmain. It belongs to Mark Hauser. It appears he's the one.'

'Well that's good. Have you got anything from him?' she asked.

'Yes, we managed to get a name from Hauser. His name is Gregory Hughes,' Mick explained. There was a slight pause.

'Bloody oath. Mick, the President is set to go on stage at the Opera House in the next hour. We've got to stop this attack,' she said.

'I know. I'll get Detectives Cooper and Faulkner working up Hughes to see if they can get a read on him,' he said.

'Fine, just do what you have to,' she finished and hung up.

****

Despite it being Australia Day and the fact that a major event was taking place at the Sydney Opera House, not everyone was celebrating. Karl Benedict, a man in his mid-fifties, was enjoying a late breakfast at one of Sydney's high-end restaurants. Karl was a businessman and the Chief Executive Officer of a multi-billion dollar company. Standing nearby were several of his private security who accompanied him wherever he went. Karl was cutting into his

Eggs Benedict and sipped on a Latte. He was also expecting to meet someone this morning for a meeting. They were running late and Karl hated it when people were late for meetings. Finally, a woman came over and sat down on the seat opposite Karl. She wore a dark blue power suit and carried a shoulder bag which she placed by her feet. It was Anna Mackenzie, the Chief Inspector of the Organised Crime Squad. She removed her sunglasses as she sat down. 'You're late, Mackenzie,' said Karl, as he took a mouthful of eggs. A waitress came over to pour her a glass of water.

'You do realise my position in the Force? I can't just up and leave whenever you request,' she replied. Karl glared at her.

'You're forgetting that large sum of money that lands in your bank account every month,' he said. Anna closed her eyes. 'I want updates.'

'I've been informed that Detective Greer is on the case. He's working with Murphy,' she added. Karl didn't reply straight away.

'I see…And Detective Greer. Is he willing to look the other way as you did?' Anna paused before responding.

'Unfortunately, not. Greer is a professional. He's by the book. If he found out Murphy and myself are working for you, he will go straight to Mick.' Karl took a sip of his latte.

'That is unfortunate…What about Greer? Will he be bought?' Anna shook her head.

'I've been informed that Detective Greer and your operative, Shane Murphy went to Hauser's place…It appears Hauser told Greer about Greg Hughes,' she said. 'He didn't reveal what he was doing, but a name is enough.' Karl didn't say anything and continued eating. 'You know everything relies on this operation succeeding?'

'I'm aware of the consequences, Mackenzie. The President will be taken out. I've just received word that our man is in possession of the device,' he said.

'That's good to hear...I still can't believe it's come to this. You know Greer is going to do everything he can to stop this from happening?'

'Of course, but by the time he figures out what's going on, it'll be too late,' said Karl. Anna didn't say anything after that.

John was in a daze as he sat in the car that was driving him back to the city. That was where he was meeting Andrew. He couldn't believe it. After all these months of being looked at as a fool by his wife and anyone he told, he was finally seeing a chance for clarity, and everything was happening at the same time. They stopped outside the main entrance to one of Canberra's most popular and busiest restaurant. Mitch slowed down and pulled over to the side of the road in an empty parking space. He climbed out and opened the door for John. He followed Mitch up the main steps and they entered an albeit empty restaurant where they would meet his son in-law. The place was a hive for politicians to have lunch meetings and to go there for a casual drink on the evenings. On a day such as this, it was bustling and active, which was why Andrew had picked it. As John and Mitch stood in the elevator taking them up, Mitch began to talk.

'Sir, if I may...I don't think this is such a good idea.' John chuckled and waved a hand dismissively. The thought of Andrew hurting someone was ridiculous now that he thought about it.

'I'll be okay, Mitch. It's nothing at all,' he said. 'It might also be best if you wait here. Andy sounded spooked on the phone.' Mitch felt a bit uncomfortable about that, but he didn't really have much choice.

'Yes Sir,' was the quiet reply. They entered

into the restaurant and immediately spotted Andrew sitting at a table. The young man was looking out of place with the way he kept on looking over his shoulder every other second. It was in contrast with the relaxed and celebratory mood in the place. He walked closer and John sat across the table from him.

'John.' John kept a level stare. 'Thanks for coming,' he said.

'It's my pleasure…So, what's with all the cloak and dagger?'

'You know Angela was an investigative journalist?' John slowly nodded. 'Well, two months before her death, she came home one night to tell me that she was on the verge of publishing a major story. But she seemed terrified about it,' he began.

'Terrified by what?'

'She said she found out that Karl Benedict was directly responsible for the murder of two people.' John's eyes widened.

'Bloody hell. Karl Benedict is this nation's biggest criminal warlord,' he said and Andrew nodded.

'Yes. She told me that Karl murdered two people because they refused to repay the money owed to him. There was also something to do with drugs, but Angela didn't get to explain that part. She said that Karl was looking to hire a professional assassin, possibly to take out the President,' said Andrew. John couldn't believe what he was hearing.

'This is insane…How can they get away with something like this?' said John.

'It's unclear, but you know how powerful and corrupt Karl Benedict is. She had enough evidence to publicly destroy him ten times over…Someone must've found out what she was doing and…Well, you know,' he said, getting emotional and teary.

'I know, Andy. It's hard…You told me someone paid you off. Was it Benedict?'

'Yeah. Before she died, Angela gave me the evidence she'd acquired against him and his organization. It was a direct statement from a witness to the murders,' Andy explained. 'Benedict's thugs paid me a visit and offered me the two hundred thousand dollars in exchange for the evidence, and to keep my mouth shut, otherwise, they'd do the same thing to me.' John didn't know what to say. 'But being intelligent as she was, Angela made a backup copy of the evidence. It was hidden in a safety deposit box in her name. I only just found the key,' he said.

'So, you have the evidence with you now?' Andrew looked around to check if they were being watched. Then, he produced a small thumb drive.

'This has the evidence against Karl Benedict. If we can get this to the right people, we can bring this bastard to justice,' he said.

'My God...And all this time I was forced to

believe my daughter committed suicide, and that she was a drug addict,' he said, as he sat there feeling overwhelmed by all of this.

'I know, I wanted to say something earlier, but I was afraid they were watching me,' said Andy.

'It's okay, Andy. You did the right thing…I'm going to expose this evidence,' he said, and Andy smiled. Mitch Clark was standing by the elevator, watching as John was talking with Andrew Shaw.

As he waited, he took out his mobile to dial a number.

'Yes?'

'It's Clark…We've got a problem.'

'And that is?'

'John Bradley, Sir, the President's husband…He's looking into his daughter's suicide again. He's meeting with the fiancé, Andrew Shaw. I think he just gave him something that may be the evidence his daughter had,' said Mitch. There was a slight pause.

'I thought we handled the Bradley situation?'

'I thought so too. But the fiancé approached him. If he goes public with that evidence, the company will be finished, Sir,' said Mitch.

'I'm aware of the consequences, Mr. Clark...See that the problem is taken care of.' Mitch paused for a moment.

'Yes, Sir,' he said, and then hung up. He continued to stand there and watch John talking with Andrew Shaw.

****

There were literally hundreds of people at the Sydney Opera House. They were all standing around the main steps where a staging area had been set up for the President of Australia to give her speech. Helicopters were flying overhead and captured breathtaking shots. A giant Australian flag was hung off the Sydney Harbour Bridge, of course, it was the new Australian republic flag, which was chosen by a separate referendum. The new flag was split into two colours; on one side was blue with the stars of the Southern Cross. On the middle section was a yellow kangaroo and behind it was a green background. Music was playing as people waited for the arrival of the President of Australia. A news reporter was standing near the entrance and was giving a live update on the event, stating that it was an overwhelming experience. Just then, the black Range Rover Sports arrived on time. It was carrying the President of Australia, Charmaine Bradley. People were screaming with excitement as they waved their own flags. A bodyguard opened the rear door. Seconds later, Charmaine Bradley emerged. The crowd erupted as she started waving at everyone. She had a big smile on her face and began walked towards the stage. Of course, the crowds were blocked off by security fences, but that didn't stop Charmaine from mixing with her supporters. She shook hands with dozens of people, the whole time she walked towards the stage.

After Mark Hauser was taken into custody, more police vehicles showed up at the property in Balmain where Mark Hauser lived. Several uniformed police officers were searching the property as well as setting up police tape around the front gate to prevent anyone from entering or leaving that weren't permitted. Inside the house, forensic officers and other detectives were taking photos of the body and blood that stained the floor. It was a major crime scene. Shane Murphy was talking to one of the officers, while Detective Sergeant Mick Greer was on the phone with Felicity Meyers, the Squad's Technical Specialist. She was at the computer typing away as she spoke. 'Any luck with the search on that name, Greg Hughes?'

'I've done a complete search of our data base, plus ASIO's, but it's pulled up nothing so far. Are you sure he said Hughes?'

'Yes, Hauser confirmed it was something to do with Greg Hughes. He's definitely involved somehow, we just have to keep digging,' said Mick. 'Try searching through the AFP's database.'

'I don't have the necessary clearance code for that network,' said Felicity.

'Hang on.' Mick checked his phone. He brought up a second screen to look for a code. 'Try AFP001579,' he said. There was a pause as Felicity typed it in. The computer beeped.

'It worked. I'm in. Starting a search now,' she said.

'Good. Call me as soon as you get something.' Then Mick hung up.

****

John had lost count of how many times he had been sent into a daze by revelations just today but as he sat in the car being driven by Mitch. He had a feeling that the day still had more revelations in store for him. Mitch was driving him to a place where they could find out what was on the USB device. He knew he should call Charmaine to tell her about it, but it would only upset her, and she must be at the Opera House by now, he realized. Angela had been killed, and he was right this whole time! He was not going crazy as the others had thought. He had been killed. John Bradley didn't know whether to cry or to laugh. He couldn't understand his emotions as he sat staring at his hands. Whatever was on this device in his hands, it had to be the most incriminating evidence for them to have gone to such lengths to keep the story from going live. He was nervous, and he was wondering if he should even open it. But he was the husband of the President. Nobody would dare to touch him, John reasoned. He was woken from his reverie by Mitch's voice from the front seat. 'We're here, Sir.' They got down and as they headed inside to see the computer specialist Mitch had talked about, Mitch cleared his throat and spoke. 'Sir, do you think this is such a good idea? I mean, finding out what's on the device?' He asked, concerned.

'Yes. I am going to expose this company and destroy them. They have to pay. They must pay for what they did to my Angela.' John said firmly, leaving the bodyguard no other choice but to nod. As Mitch opened the door for him to enter, John stepped inside to freeze in shock. The blood drained from his face as he registered what he was seeing. Right in the middle of the living room, there was a body lying in a rapidly spreading pool of blood. Quickly, he reached over to check if the person was alive when he froze again. It was actually Andrew lying there, stabbed multiple times with his breath coming in ragged gasps. His eyes looked like they wanted to warn John, but his body wouldn't obey him. 'Quick, Mitch! Call an ambulance!'

John turned to shout at the bodyguard who had just entered the room. Mitch Clark had a gun in his hand, pointed straight at the First Gentleman of the country. There was a stoic expression on his face as he released the guard on the gun. 'W-what are you doing, Mitch? Mitch? What's this, why are you doing this?' John asked, the incredibility of the situation staring him right in the face. Mitch shook his head. 'I tried to discourage you. I really tried, Sir. I have no choice but to do this now.' John was sitting there, shaking in fear.

'I work for Birchall McClelland, Sir. I've been

working for them for a while now. We believe that this country needs a better hand to steer it to greatness, and that what we're doing…We're doing what's right for Australia.' He continued.

'Wait...D-does that mean...It was you!' John accused in rage. 'It was you who killed Angela!' Mitch only nodded solemnly as he slowly said without hesitation, 'She inherited your determination, Sir. For what it's worth, she died quickly. She didn't suffer.' John slowly stood up, staring down the muzzle of the gun in trepidation for his life. He would never have believed the day's events would come to such a conclusion.

Mick Greer and Shane Murphy were driving through the city. Their police lights were flashing and the siren was blaring. He wasn't waiting around for anyone. Just then, Mick's phone started ringing. 'Go ahead,' he answered, putting it on speaker.

'Boss, I got something on Greg Hughes. He's a mercenary and currently working as a freelancer for Karl Benedict.' Mick looked at Shane.

'Bloody hell. Does he have any known

associates?' asked Mick.

'Yes, I came across another name…Nathaniel Manson. Apparently they were colleagues in the Army twenty years ago. Manson defected from the Army in 2005. He then resurfaced as a mercenary, also working for Benedict,' Felicity explained.

'Shit. Looks like these guys are professional. Any idea where they are now?'

'No. They're mercenaries, they're trained to stay off the grid.'

'Damn it.'

'There's one other thing…Hughes worked in the Army as a Bomb Disposal Officer. He was trained to disarm explosive devices and served in Afghanistan and Iraq.'

'My God…So Hauser must've given these guys legitimate security passes so they could gain access to the Opera House?' Mick thought.

'It looks like it,' said Felicity as she looked at her screen.

'Son of a bitch...Okay, call security at the Opera House, tell them they have a security breach. Also, call Detective Mackenzie, get her to send extra backup.'

'Copy that.' The call disconnected. Mick put his foot down on the accelerator.

****

With five minutes of shaking hands and getting photos taken done, Charmaine Bradley finally made her way into the Opera House. She was giving her speech in the main concert hall in front of hundreds of people. She along with Joe Parsons and her staff made their way into the building. Security lined the main corridor leading to the concert hall. Charmaine's heart was racing the whole time she got nearer to the doors. As she got to the door, a man standing there waiting. He was the manager of the Opera House and he shook her hand. She smiled and introduced herself and Joe Parsons. The manager then led them in through the doors. She was then greeted by the Governor of New South Wales, Brendan King. The audience was already cheering and waving their flags as they saw the President. The Governor smiled at Charmaine as they shook hands. Charmaine had a big smile on her face. The Governor then turned and stood in front of the podium that was placed at the front of the main stage. 'Ladies and gentlemen...I'd like to welcome to the stage, the first President of Australia, our very own Australian head of state...Charmaine Bradley!' said the Governor. The audience erupted with a round of applause and continued shouting and whistling. Charmaine shook hands with the Governor once more and she gave him a kiss on the cheek. She stepped up to the podium and stood there for a few moments as the audience continued to go wild. She could barely get a word in. At last, they all started to settle down.

'Fellow Australians!' she said. Again, the crowd cheered and whistled. 'Thank you all for coming out here on such a beautiful day,' she began. 'I can't begin to tell you how proud and honoured I am to be here today,' she added. Joe Parsons was standing to the left of the stage and watched on as Charmaine spoke. 'I was humbled, and certainly proud to be offered the opportunity to serve you, the Australian people, as your first head of state,' she said. 'I couldn't believe it when I heard the referendum to become a republic was a complete success...I was especially proud and privileged to give this speech on this day, January 26th, marking the anniversary of the 1788 arrival of the First Fleet of British ships at Port Jackson, and the raising of the flag of Great Britain at Sydney Cove.' The crowd was captivated by the President's speech. 'I would like to take this opportunity to show how grateful I am to be the first President of Australia…To be the first citizen to hold the highest office in all the land, and to be witness to the birth of a new era in history!' she shouted. More cheers and whistles were made. Joe knew that Charmaine was wrapping up her speech. As he stood there listening, Joe felt his phone vibrating. He quickly took it out to answer the incoming call. 'Joe Parsons!' he shouted, holding one finger against his ear. It was quite loud trying to hear who was on the other end.

'Mr. Parsons, this is Chief Inspector Anna Mackenzie again,' said Anna.

'What's going on, Ms. Mackenzie?' he remembered who she was from the last time they spoke.

'I'm calling to alert you to a situation. We've just found evidence the President is in imminent danger,' he said. Joe's eyes widened.

'Say that again?'

'I said, the President's life is in danger! You

need to evacuate the President, now!' said Anna.

'Ms. Mackenzie, the President is on stage giving her speech, I can't just drag her off,' he said.

'Sir, the President's life is at stake. You need to get her out of there, now!' she shouted. Joe stood there and hesitated. He then looked back at Charmaine, who was standing there smiling and waving. Charmaine Bradley was wrapping up her speech. The audience was ecstatic as she spoke and kept waving their flags. Charmaine's heart was pounding rapidly. She stopped for a moment and let the crowd cheer. She had a big smile on her face. 'And so, it is my greatest honour to be given this opportunity to serve you as Australia's first President!' she said. 'May God bless you all and God bless the Republic of Australia!' she finished. Everyone cheered again, and Charmaine started waving. The Prime Minister of Australia stepped forward and clapped his hands as he approached Charmaine. The Australian national anthem began to play through the loudspeakers. She turned, and they shook hands.

John Bradley was lying on the floor. Blood everywhere around him. He'd been shot, but he was still alive, barely. Mitch Clark, the man who shot him, was walking around him, like a lion circling his caught pray. As he walked around, he took out his mobile to dial a number. 'Mr. Benedict, it's Mitch Clark.'

'Is the job done?'

'Yes, Sir. Mr. Bradley is out of the picture. He won't be causing us any problems,' said Mitch.

'That's good to hear, Mitch. Your payment

will be wired to your usual account,' said Karl Benedict. Mitch grinned, then he hung up. He looked down at John Bradley who was lying there, bleeding to death. He did feel bad for him. But Mitch was hired to do a job. But he decided to do the right thing. He started dialling a number. 'Ambulance please…John Bradley has been shot, I need ambulance and police here at 47 Victor Street, Yarralumla. Get here as soon as you can!' he shouted.

****

Mick Greer and Shane Murphy finally arrived at the Opera House. They pulled up near the main entrance and got out of the car. As they did, they both withdrew their handguns. At the same time, they showed the security officers their IDs and were allowed through. They ran up the stairs to the main entrance. They made it to the concert hall where they were stopped by the President's head of security. 'I'm Detective Senior Sergeant Mick Greer, Organised Crime Squad. You need to get the President out of here, now!' he said.

'What's going on?' asked the head of security, Jim Ross.

'There's a threat to the President's life. We need to evacuate this building now,' said Mick.

****

Charmaine turned to the audience who were cheering and waving their flags. She raised her hand to give a wave. She had a big smile on her face. At that, there was a massive explosion. A bomb had gone off in the van that Greg and his men arrived in. The explosion ripped through the main concert hall, throwing chunks of concrete. The force of the explosion knocked Charmaine to the floor and she was covered by falling debris. The explosion was massive. It ripped through the side of the Opera House causing severe damage to the building. Inside the main concert hall, there was a thick layer of smoke and lung-choking dust. A fire alarm was echoing throughout the building. It was loud and ear piercing. People were screaming as they were trapped by the semi-collapsed ceiling. On the stage, Charmaine Bradley had been knocked to the floor. She was covered by a large amount of concrete and she'd been knocked unconscious. There were several other people on the stage, one being the Governor, the other being the Prime Minister of Australia. About six of the President's security personnel managed to get inside the destroyed hall. They found the President and paramedics came racing over to give her medical assistance. She was alive but was injured from the debris. She had cuts and bruises over her head and arms. The paramedics checked her over and managed to find a pulse. They quickly got her onto a stretcher and carried her outside. More paramedics and rescue workers started to arrive and went into the building to search for survivors.

****

There were no words to describe how Mick Greer was feeling right now. He just couldn't believe what had happened. He pulled up in a parking space at the New South Wales Police Force headquarters in Parramatta' underground garage. He turned off the engine and sat there still in complete shock. On the way over, he'd been listening to the radio about the horrifying terrorist attack on the Sydney Opera House. The report went on to state that it was a national tragedy and that the nation will be mourning the loss of so many innocent lives. Eventually, Mick found the strength to make his way into the building. The elevator took him up to the fifth floor and he stepped onto the

Operations Centre of the Organised Crime Squad. As he walked across the main floor, he could see everyone standing at their workstations. They were looking in complete horror at the large screen; it was displaying a live news report on the bomb attack. Mick made his way over to Anna Mackenzie's office. He knocked twice and after pausing, he showed himself in. Anna was there talking on the phone to someone. 'Yes, thank you for informing me. I appreciate that, Assistant Commissioner,' she said, before hanging up. 'Detective Greer, do come in.'

'Boss, I can't believe this happened,' he said.

'Yes, I know. It's horrible. Still nothing on the man behind the attack,' she said. There was a pause and Anna closed her eyes in disbelief.

'What's happening with Hauser?' asked Mick, changing the subject.

'The suspect you arrested has been brought in by Tactical Response. He's in the holding room waiting to be questioned,' said Anna and Mick nodded.

'What's the status of the President?'

'She's alive, thankfully. Her injuries weren't as severe as doctors thought, so she's been taken to Canberra for additional security,' she explained. 'I've also been informed that upwards of fifty were killed in the blast.'

'Shit,' Mick cursed. Anna didn't say anything after that.

'Gentlemen, the meeting will now come to order.' Fourteen men had gathered in the main board room. The board room was located on the top floor of the Birchall McClelland office. The BMC office was located in Sydney, the flagship headquarters of the organisation and occupied two thirds of the Governor Phillip Tower in Sydney's financial district. The building stood an impressive two hundred and twenty seven metres into the air and was one of the tallest buildings in the city. The board room was set up just like any ordinary executive office boardroom. In the centre was a large square-shaped table with fifteen executive office chairs around it. Of course, one of them was at the front, reserved for the Chairman of the Board. Ten of the men sat in padded office chairs around the conference table. The men represented various intelligence organizations and branches of the Australian defence department. Against one wall, four more men sat in folding chairs. These men represented four broad civilian industries, including coal mining, oil and natural gas, banking and finance, and aerospace and defence. The group operated in secrecy, even from itself. No one in the room wore identifying markers of any kind. There were no name plates, no indications of rank, and no combat ribbons or medals in evidence. Indeed, there were no uniforms. The military men all wore dress shirts and slacks.

Although most of the men knew one another to some degree, two of the men were strangers, and had affiliations that were unclear to the rest of the group. A silver-haired, four-star general, once a commander in the Army, stood at the head of the table. He rubbed an old, long faded scar on his forehead. It was Karl Benedict, the Chief Executive Officer of Birchall McClelland. 'You all know me,' he said. 'You know my role here. So, I'll get right to it. Events have moved forward quickly in the past twenty-four-hours, faster than we could have anticipated. I realise that past events were supposed to show this country that we mean business…However, it would seem that it's not the case,' said Karl Benedict. 'I know that you're all against the idea of this country becoming a republic, and I know that you're all aware that two days ago, there was a successful attack on the President of Australia,' said Karl. 'I'd like to assure you all here today, that I, Karl Benedict, the Chief

Executive Officer of Birchall McClelland, has sworn an oath to protect the Australian people from this disaster,' said Karl. There was an eerie silence in the room as he looked around at all the members. A hand at the table was raised. Karl recognized a man much older than himself, a former Royal Australian Navy admiral. There was an iconic photograph from the event, which had never been declassified, but which the general had seen. It showed the admiral at nineteen years of age, shirtless in a muddy trench, his eyes wild, his face and upper body painted dark red with the blood of dead communists. 'Yes?' Mr. Benedict asked.

'Just what exactly are you proposing, Mr. Benedict?' asked one of the members. Karl didn't reply straight away, and he grinned. 'I appreciate your curiosity. What I am proposing, will change this country.'

'Do you anticipate that it will cause any problems?' said another member. Karl picked up the paper in front of him and began to carefully shred it into long narrow strips.

'We don't anticipate,' he said, 'any problems at all.' There was silence across the room. 'Now, moving on...According to my notes, some of you have expressed concerns with this operation,' he said. 'Let me assure you, that this operation will help ensure the safety and the future of the Australian government...I realize that it is a drastic measure, to allow terrorists to carry out attacks on Australian soil, but we need to show this government is weak, and the Australian people deserve better,' he said. 'I believe that a regime change in this country will make it stronger, and we can achieve those goals...Let's stand together, and let's make Australia great again!' the others around the table started clapping. The board meeting ended. All the executives started making their way out of the dull, boring room, and headed back to their offices. Karl Benedict remained in his comfortable chair, feeling regal and impressed with himself. He sat there going over some paperwork and his notes on the meeting. Just then, his Executive Assistant entered. She approached him with caution. 'Excuse me, Mr. Benedict. There's a Mr. Clark here to see you,' she said. Karl immediately looked up, surprised. 'He's here now?' she slowly nodded. 'Son of a bitch...Send him in,' he demanded. She quickly raced off to carry out his command. A few moments later, Mitch Clark, the personal bodyguard to John Bradley, entered the room. 'What the fuck are you doing here?' Mitch was a little thrown off by his response.

'I apologise for the interruption. I couldn't get a hold of you,' said Mitch, bravely. Karl let out a sigh.

'Your movements are supposed to be discrete. I can't have you wandering about the office. This is supposed to be a clandestine operation,' he said.

'The operation was a complete success, Mr. Benedict…You got what you wanted, now I want what I wanted…My payment and a one-way ticket out of this bloody country,' said Mitch. Karl didn't look too impressed.

'I see…Well, your payment was wired to your account,' said Karl. 'As for your travel arrangements…They will be handled by another associate of mine…Head to this address. He'll meet you there to make sure you get out of the country,' said Karl. He then handed Mitch a piece of paper. He took it and checked the address.

He didn't say anything after that. He nodded and then got up to leave. After he left, Karl picked up the phone and dialled a number. 'It's me…He's on his way…Make sure you take care of it,' he ordered, and then hung up the call. Karl went back to watching the large TV screen.

****

The nation was in complete shock right now. They couldn't believe there was a deadly terrorist attack the Australia Day festival. The attack took place at the Sydney Opera House, moments after the President had finished her speech. A black Range Rover with official government number plates pulled onto the tarmac at Sydney Airport. Charmaine Bradley, the President of Australia, sat in the back seat of the Range Rover. Charmaine was still in shock by what happened, which was understandable, considering she'd just survived a terrorist attack. She had cuts and bruises all over her face and a massive gash along the side of her arm where she fell and was hit by some falling debris. Thankfully, her injuries weren't as severe, but others weren't so lucky. The car pulled up alongside the Australian Air Force Boeing 787 and Charmaine's driver got out. He opened the door, allowing her to climb out. She was currently running on autopilot. Her entire body was numb from the shock, which was only natural. She was led onto the aircraft by her security detail. Joe Parsons followed closely by her. Not a single word was spoken as they headed up the metal stairs and boarded the aircraft. She was led down the narrow aisle to her private office. It was only then that Joe spoke up and wanted to know if she was okay. 'Is there anything I can get you, Madam President?' he asked, softly, as he closed the door. Charmaine didn't respond straight away. She sat down at her large desk and buried her head in her hands.

'I still can't believe something like this happened,' she said, with a sob. A tear trickled down her cheek. Joe hesitated before replying.

'I know. It was horrible…There's a paramedic coming to check you out and to clean up those wounds,' said Joe. Charmaine didn't say anything to that.

'How the hell did this happen, Joe?' he paused.

'I'm still not quite sure myself, Ma'am. I believe the AFP is still investigating.' She looked at the TV that was on in the office. It showed an aerial shot of the Opera House and the news reporter was giving an update on the terrorist attack. While she was still getting over the ordeal of the attack, she had to remain focused and get into the habit of running the country.

'I just can't get over the fact that something like this happened,' she said.

'I completely understand…Is there anything I can get you?' he asked. She paused for a moment.

'I'd like a coffee actually,' she said. Just then, there was gentle knock on the door. An Air Force Officer stepped in.

'Madam President, we're about to take off,' he said, and Charmaine nodded. The President was being taken back to Canberra as it was deemed unsafe for her to remain in Sydney.

After the catastrophic attack at the Sydney Opera House, Shane Murphy headed back to his place in Sydney's Bondi Beach. He owned a luxurious studio townhouse that he bought outright twelve months ago. The advantages of having a well-paying job, however, it did have its drawbacks. For instance, he had no idea his job would result in the loss of so many innocent people. He couldn't believe that the bomb actually went off, and all those people were killed. Not to mention the Prime Minister of Australia. He was frustrated by the fact that he worked for these people, but not that he really had much choice. He was basically forced into the position. Shane was glad that he reached out to his friend, Mick Greer though, as he felt it was important to stop these people. Shane slumped down on his couch and started enjoying a nice cold beer. He still had dust all over his clothes from when the bomb went off. He had cuts and bruises from the falling debris. But he didn't care. He just sat there feeling completely shattered as he sipped his drink. He flipped the TV on and saw there was a news report of the horrifying events that took place at the Opera House. The report was showing people running in all directions. A plume of smoke rose into the air where the bomb tore through the building. Shane couldn't believe he helped these guys do this. All those people were killed, because of him. He sat there on the couch, feeling a bit shellshocked as a result. As he sat there watching in horror, his eyes widened at the sound of a knock on the door. He waited a moment to see if it went away, but there was another knock. He quickly got up to mute the TV and headed over to the front door. Carefully, he took out his gun and hid it behind his back. 'Who is it?' Shane called out.

'It's Clark. Benedict sent me,' he said. Shane paused for a moment and then unlocked the door. Sure enough, Mitch Clark was standing there in the doorway.

'Come in,' he said, softly. When Mitch stepped in, Shane quickly closed the door.

'Benedict told me you could help me leave the country?' he asked.

'Yes, I can arrange for you to get to Indonesia. From there, you'll be able to seek amnesty,' said Shane.

'Sounds like a plan…When do I leave?' he asked. Shane didn't respond straight away. He thought for a moment and caught the news report in the corner of his eye. He saw the devastating results of the bomb attack. He then turned to Mitch.

'Soon…So, you were Bradley's bodyguard?' he asked, changing the subject. Mitch slowly nodded.

'Yes…I had to take him out though, he was getting close to finding out who really killed his daughter,' he said. Shane didn't know what to say to that.

'Alright then…There's just one problem…When I spoke to Benedict, he gave me orders…To kill you.' There was a brief pause. If Shane were a slower human by the fracture of the second it took him to sidestep the attack, he would have been clutching at a crushed windpipe. But Shane faced down deadlier and faster men than Mitch. His feral, baser instincts kicked in, and the fighter in him came to play. Mitch was fast, he had to give him that, in the space of five seconds, he had sent eleven blows Mitch's way, and each of them were killer blows in their own right. The kitchen space naturally provided its own theatre for battle, complete with props. So, it was no surprise that a large cutting knife appeared in Mitch's hand. Shane watched him jostle the knife from hand to hand and he knew it was to demoralise him. He realised Mitch did not only learn to fight, but he also learned to fight dirty. Mitch assumed a death strike stance with the knife tip pointed at Shane's belly. Shane knew that move. If Mitch was proficient with it as the Japanese masters who had perfected it for centuries, Shane knew there was no escaping. He could only hope Mitch wasn't very proficient or better still he could find a shield. His hand reached for the frying pan hung on the wall behind him.

'It's funny…Benedict gave me the same orders,' said Mitch. He lunged with all his might. He was a blur until Shane heard steel hit steel as the knife dented the base of the pan. He saw an opening in the split second and brought his knee up as hard as he could. It caught Mitch smack in the jaw and he heard him grunt as he fell. The knife clattered from his hand but he was on his feet again. Prancing from one foot to the other. His fist bunched and his jaw set. Shane had to use the small window to reposition himself to gain more space advantage. Mitch threw a fast punch for Shane's face. He didn't dodge. He allowed it to hit him because he knew it was not the punch that would cause him to fall. It was the second one that came a second after. And it was that he parried. It was aimed at his sternum. If it had hit home, Shane knew he would be on the floor. He realised he had been combating Mitch on the defensive. Now, he knew he had to attack or else things would get really out of hand. Shane had spent a full year at a Kung Fu dojo and had obtained the sixth Wu Shu. He knew what Mitch needed and that was what he was going to give. He let out his open palm in attack. It was coming in as a frontal slap. It would have been comical if it wasn't one of the most cunning and deadliest blows. It was aimed for the entire face of the opponent. It was to obliterate the line of vision of the opponent while the real blow came in. In the microsecond Mitch was momentarily limited to seeing Shane's palm, he felt a sharp pain in his belly and groin and chest almost at the same time. He crumpled on the floor. It felt as though a train had run at him. His body was on fire. What the hell was that? That couldn't have been from only one person and certainly not the work of a single human hand. He had never faced such a blow in his entire life of fighting. And there he was on his parent's kitchen floor groaning from a blow he didn't even see. He looked up to see Mitch's shoed foot coming to his face. Just before he was about to get an imprint of his shoe, Shane grabbed hold of Mitch's ankle, and twisted it. This action forced his body to collapse to the ground. His head smacked hard on the tiled floor. Blood started pouring from the wound. Shane took a moment to collect himself, and then looked over to see Mitch lying there, choking to death. There was a giant puddle of blood surrounding his cranium. He couldn't believe what'd happened. Karl must've wanted him dead, but for what reason? He had to find out. Despite being in shock, the adrenalin rush from the fight was kicking in. He went over to Mitch's now dead body and started searching through his pockets. He found his wallet, phone and a small envelope. Checking inside, he saw a USB thumb drive. It must be what John Bradley had before he too was killed. He grabbed it and went over to his computer, plugging it in at the same time. He was excited, but also shit scared at the same time. As he waited for the USB drive to boot up on his computer, he got out his phone to make a call. It kept ringing a few times before it finally answered.

'Mick Greer.'

'Mick, it's Shane…I need your help.'

'Shane? What's wrong? Where are you?'

'I'm at my apartment, but I need your help on something. It's important.' There was a brief pause followed by a sigh.

'I'm about to go and question Mark Hauser to find out what he knows,' said Mick.

'Yes, but this is more important. Please, Mick. I helped you get to Mark Hauser. Benedict just tried to have me killed,' he said.

'Shit…Okay, where are you now?'

'I'm at my apartment. I sent the address to your phone already,' he said.

'Okay. I'll be there in ten minutes.' Shane hung up the phone. He was staring at the screen and couldn't believe what he was seeing.

Shane Murphy couldn't believe that he'd just survived a hit. More to the fact that Karl Benedict wanted him dead. It just didn't make sense; if anything, Mitch was the one who needed to be taken out. Shane was sitting on the couch, drinking a beer to calm his nerves after the brutal punch up. Mitch's body lay on the floor, blood surrounding it. He just didn't know what to do. He knew he had to call the police, and an ambulance to come and collect the body, but he just couldn't do it. He couldn't risk it. Instead, he called someone else to come. Mick

Greer came in through the front door of the townhouse. The moment he stepped inside, it looked as though the place had been burgled. Shattered glass lay all over the floor. As he got further into the kitchen, he noticed blood. Then, he spotted the body. 'Shane?' Mick spoke, softly. 'Shane, you there?'

'Yeah, I'm in the lounge,' he called out. His voice was very faint, obviously from the shock. Mick came into the lounge, and found Shane on the couch, his clothes covered in blood.

'Shit. Are you okay?' asked Mick, becoming concerned.

'I think so. Just in a bit of shock, that's all,' he said.

'What the hell happened? Who is this guy?' Mick indicated to the dead body.

'His name is Mitch Clark. He was John Bradley's personal bodyguard,' Shane explained, slowly. He slowly managed to get to his feet, but his legs were like jelly. Mick helped him up.

'So why did he end up a corpse?'

'Looks like Benedict is trying to tie off loose ends…There's something else you need to see.' Shane led him over to his computer.

'What is it?' Shane brought up several files and images to go with them.

'Turns out Bradley's daughter, Angela, was trying to bring BMC down. She'd acquired proof that BMC murdered two people. They were in a position to go public with the fact that Birchall McClelland were corrupt,' he said. Mick's eyes suddenly widened as he saw what was on the screen. He couldn't believe what he was looking at.

'Jesus fuck…I can't believe this.'

'I know…One this for sure, Birchall McClelland are pure evil,' he said. There was a brief pause.

'This is fucking insane…You're saying that an Australian private defence contractor, one of the largest in the Oceanic region, is responsible for the assassination attempt on the President of Australia?' Mick thought.

'It's a high probability…I know it's hard to believe, but Mitch's attempt to kill me should prove it. And the fact that he's an AFP agent,' said Shane.

'It's not going to convince the High Courts though. We'll need hard evidence to bring these guys down if they are responsible.'

'I know they're responsible, Mick. I've been working for them for the past two years. I know what they're capable of,' he said. Mick didn't know what to say after that. Just then, Shane could hear a buzzing noise coming from Mitch's pocket. He crouched down and carefully reached into his pocket to take out his Smartphone. The phone was ringing, but the number had an 'unknown caller' ID.

'It must be his employer, Birchall McClelland,' said Mick, as they stared at the phone.

'What should I do?' said Shane. Then, without hesitation, he answered the call. 'Yes?'

'Congratulations, Murphy…You're finally solving the puzzle,' said a deep voice on the other end. Shane looked confused.

'Benedict? Why the fuck did you try to kill me?' he asked.

'No matter what you do, you'll never be able to bring this company down,' said the voice. At that, the call disconnected. Seconds later, Shane looked up to the sound of screeching tires. He raced to the door, and at the last second, he spotted a vehicle speeding off. Mick came out after him.

'Looks like you were being watched,' said Mick.

'It would seem that way…Mick, this thing is huge. We need to find out who exactly is involved in this conspiracy, and what BMC are planning,' said Shane. Mick slowly nodded, then looked at the blood on Shane's clothes and hands.

'We also need to deal with that corpse,' he said. He paused for a moment, before taking out his mobile phone. 'I know someone who I can get to come take care of it. We'll cover it up, make it look like a suicide,' he added. At that, Mick's phone started ringing. 'Detective Greer.' Shane stood there, feeling overwhelmed by all of this. 'Okay, I'll be there soon.' He hung up the call. 'That was the office. Hauser is ready to be interviewed,' he said. 'Look, I need to see this through. Obviously, we can't bring you in, because Benedict will know, and you're a suspect in a murder case...' Shane didn't know what to say. 'You can stay at my place for the time being, until we can get this thing sorted.'

'Thanks, Mick. I really appreciate you helping,' he said.

'No problem, that's what friends are for, right?' Then, they made their way over to

Mick's car and drove off.

****

The Boeing 787 with Air Force markings on it, touched down at Canberra Airport. It taxied to the Air Force section of the airport where a set of vehicles were parked waiting. Once the aircraft stopped, Charmaine and her staff deboarded the plane. She climbed down the stairs and got into the vehicle which had its door open already. Joe followed behind her and got into the seat next to her. Charmaine Bradley, the President of Australia, was tired. It had been a long, trying day for the nation's first President. Not surprising, considering what she'd been through. First, she survived a catastrophic terrorist attack that resulted in the deaths of upwards of a hundred people. Then, she found out that her husband, John Bradley, was in hospital fighting for his life. Charmaine was at her desk. Her head was lying on flat on the desk and she'd been crying about John. Just then, there was a knock at the door. Joe Parsons, the President's Official Secretary entered. He carried some folders. He walked up to the President's desk and saw that she'd been crying. Not surprising to be honest. 'Madam President, can I get you anything?' he asked. She just shook her head.

'No, thank you Joe. I'm okay. Just can't believe everything that's happened. First it was the terrorist attack and now John's fighting for his right to live,' she said and Joe nodded.

'I spoke with the hospital. He's in an induced coma. Apparently the knife wound was quite severe and punctured several vital organs. It's going to be quite some time before he comes out of it,' said Joe. Charmaine closed her eyes. A tear trickled down her cheek. 'I am sorry, Ma'am.' The car was making its way into Canberra.

'It's fine, Joe. What've you got there?' she

asked, indicating to the folders under his arms.

'I've spoken with the AFP. They've finally released a full report on what happened today…But we can deal with that tomorrow. Once we get to the residence, you should get some rest, Madam President.' But Charmaine shook her head.

'No, it's fine. I want to know what happened to all those innocent people.'

'Very well.' Joe slipped on his reading glasses and opened the folder to read. 'According to the AFP, the attack on the Opera House was carried out by an IED, Improvised Explosive Device. The suspect managed to smuggle the device onto the grounds of the Opera House,' he explained.

'My God…How the hell did he do that?'

'Apparently Mr. Hughes had an accomplice who the AFP have in custody right now. He was the one who provided him with the explosive and a legitimate security card,' he said.

'This is insane...' Charmaine just sat there with her eyes closed and shook her head in disbelief. 'You should also know, the Deputy Prime Minister is here. He wants to discuss what's happening since the PM was killed in the attack,' he said.

'Is he serious? The PM's only been dead for eight hours or so,' she replied.

'I know, but the fact is, this country needs a new prime minister. And since you're the President, it's your responsibility to appoint the interim Prime Minister,' he explained. Charmaine just let out a sigh. 'At least start the dialogue with the Deputy Prime Minister.' Charmaine nodded. Then, Joe turned his head to speak with the driver. 'We're making a detour. Head to the Parliament House.' The driver nodded and then indicated to change lanes.

After a five-minute drive, the President's

escort vehicle finally arrived at the Parliament House. It pulled into the underground parking garage and drove over to the President's VIP parking spot. She had a reserved space since she was the head of state and frequently visited the Parliament House, as the Governor-General once did. As it stopped, Charmaine climbed out of the car with Joe following behind. She was escorted into the building and after making their way to the executive office wing, Charmaine found herself at the office of Deputy Prime Minister. Joe knocked on the door and opened it allowing the President to enter. Alistair Cohen, the Deputy Prime Minister of Australia, stood up as Charmaine and Joe entered.

'Good evening, Madam President,' he spoke. 'My condolences about your husband. I hope he pulls through,' said Alistair.

'Thank you, Deputy Prime Minister. He's a fighter,' said Charmaine, as they shook hands. 'I was told you wanted to discuss the vacant position of Prime Minister?' she said and Alistair nodded.

For the past several hours, Mark Hauser had been held in one of the Organised Crime Squad's holding rooms. It was a dull room with a double-sided window on one side. This was to allow detectives to monitor Hauser. He was currently sitting on a metal chair placed in the middle of the room. Ever since he was transferred here, he never spoke a word. No one seemed to be able to get any information from him. He was a criminal after all. The door to the holding room opened. Mark slowly looked up to see a man enter. It was Detective Senior Sergeant Mick Greer. He was looking rather pensive, mostly because he was annoyed by Hauser's refusal to cooperate. Mick came over and sat down on the spare chair opposite Hauser. As she sat there, Mark just gave him a cheeky grin. 'I'm glad you find this funny,' Mick said. Of course, Hauser didn't say anything. Mick had a folder with him. He opened it and laid out several images. They were images of body bags laid out on the street nearby the half destroyed Sydney Opera House. Some were small sized for children. 'Take a look at your handy work,' he began. 'We know Gregory Hughes was the one behind this attack, but you were the one who gave him a legitimate access code and the IED so he could get through security at the Opera House undetected,' said Mick, placing more images in front of Mark. He looked at them and just shrugged, as if to say, whatever. 'We searched your house. We found a large quantity of illicit substances, including weapons and a ton of cash,' said Mick. 'For that, you'll be looking at going away for quite some time. Not to mention the fact that you planned on shooting a detective,' said Mick. 'What is Benedict planning? What's his end game?' Hauser was refusing to give in. 'If you don't start cooperating, you're going to prison. Benedict won't be able to protect you, you're already a liability,' he said. Just then, Mick looked up as there was a tap on the window. He looked back as Mark chuckled. He wasn't impressed and stared at him, then stormed out. Mick made his way back into the observation room. Lead Police Detective Anna Mackenzie was there watching. Felicity Meyers was also in the room and she was monitoring Hauser's vitals. Detective Senior Constable Ethan Cooper was observing also.

'Boss, this is going nowhere,' said Mick, as he closed the door.

'I know. He's a tough bastard and I don't think the good cop bad cop routine is going to work in this situation,' said Anna. 'Did you get anything from his laptop?' she asked.

'I'm still searching through his hard drive. It's mostly junk and pornography, but I'll keep looking,' said Felicity.

'Damn it. This guy knows something. We have to figure out what his connection to all of this is,' said Mick, getting frustrated. 'Okay, keep working up on his profile, I'm going back in.'

****

Australian Army Major-General George Stanley stepped off the elevator. General Stanley was in his late forties, and several years away from hitting fifty. He was probably one of the youngest to make the rank of Major-General, but that's because he was a dedicated service man. That was until Australia became a republic; General Stanley was one of those people who hated the idea of the country being a republic. So much so that he chose to resign his post in the Australian Army. General Stanley was hired by Birchall McClelland to train other like-minded personnel. He made his way down the corridor that led him to a reception area. There was a woman behind the desk, and she smiled at the General. She didn't even bother to stop him as she knew who he was. The General entered a large office. He had a meeting with the company's Chairman, Karl Benedict; a secret meeting which only he knew about. Karl Benedict was sitting at his large glass desk. The TV was on and it displayed a news report on the recent terrorist attack on the Opera House. The attack had been churning the news cycle for the last couple of hours nonstop. General Stanley stood there and waited as his boss had his chair turned away. 'Are we on schedule?' Karl spoke finally.

'Yes Sir. I've made all the arrangements. My men are prepared and ready to move on the target,' he said. Karl smiled at that.

'Good to hear.' The chair swung around. Karl Benedict smiled at the General.

'It appears the Opera House bombing was a success,' he said, pointing to the TV.

'It was…But our target is still alive. She's a resilient bitch,' Karl snapped back. General Stanley didn't say anything to that. 'Which is why this next stage of the operation must go accordingly…I've just been informed the President is in Canberra. How long will it take to make the trip?' he asked.

'We'll be there in three hours. My men are ready to leave right now,' he said. Karl paused before responding.

'That's good, you should get on the road now…Nevertheless, this country will regret becoming a republic,' he said. General Stanley nodded. The room fell silent after that, and Karl looked back at the TV.

'I'll call you once we're in Canberra.' There was no response, which meant there was nothing more to be said. After his meeting, General Stanley made his way out of the building. Out the front of the building was a large vehicle. The General approached it and climbed into the front seat.

'What's happening, General?' asked the driver.

'We've been given the all-clear. You boys ready?' he asked. The driver nodded. He looked over his shoulder to the back where eight men were huddled in the back. They were all dressed in military gear and equipped with advanced weaponry. They all nodded at the same time. 'Right, let's rock n' roll,' he said. The driver started up the engine and slowly drove off.

Mick Greer was frustrated that Mark Hauser was refusing to cooperate. He wasn't giving up anything about his knowledge of the terrorist attack or what Karl Benedict was planning. Mark was still sitting at the metal table in the holding room. He'd been sitting there for the past hour. He glanced at the clock on the wall and saw that it was 7:15pm. He grinned, as if to know something was happening soon. Just then, the door opened and Mick stepped in again. 'Back again, Detective?' said Mark, sarcastically. Mick didn't look so impressed by what he'd just said. He walked over to the table and sat down.

'Here's how it's going to go…I'm going to offer you a deal, you're going to take that deal and then you're going to tell me everything I need to know about Karl Benedict's operation,' he said. That got Mark's attention. They must be desperate to offer him a deal.

'That's interesting…What kind of deal are we talking about?' asked Hauser.

'This agency is prepared to offer you a get-out-of-jail free card, in exchange for any information you can give us on what Karl Benedict's crew is planning,' said Mick. It was certainly an enticing deal and it would mean not spending a single day in prison.

'I see…And do you have this deal now?' said Hauser. He suspected this lower level cop needed to get authorization from higher-ups first. But, to his surprise, Mick pulled out an envelope. He opened it and inside was an official-looking piece of paper with the Department of Justice symbol at the top of it. He started reading over it. There was a signature at the bottom; it was signed by the Commissioner and authorized by the Attorney-General.

'I'm impressed…Normally this takes quite some time to slap together,' he said, knowing how slow the police usually works.

'We don't have the luxury of time. The government is prepared to honour this deal if you produce something credible,' said Mick. There was a pause in the conversation. Then Mark looked at the clock again. It was now 7:45pm.

'In the event that the President wasn't killed in the attack, Karl Benedict arranged a secondary operation,' he began.

'What kind of operation?'

'He hated the idea of Australia being a republic. So much so he was willing to kill innocent Australians to take out the President…He wants to take back this country and by doing so, he's going to take out the President.' Mick's eyes widened.

'And how exactly is he going to do that?'

'He hired a kill squad to go into the Parliament House and execute the President,' he explained. Mick's eyes widened.

'Shit…How many are in this 'kill squad?'

'It's a small team of eight men, all mercenaries and loyal to Benedict's bank account,' he said. 'They are willing to kill and they will kill anyone who gets in their way.' Mick couldn't believe what he was hearing and continued to stare at Mark Hauser.

'When is it happening?' Mark looked at the clock. It was 7:50pm now.

'Eight o'clock…' Mick's mouth lowered. He then jumped up and raced out the door.

'Detective Cooper, you're with me. Felicity, contact the President's security detail!' Mick shouted as he was making his way out the door at the same time. Ethan followed. The two detectives made their way to the rooftop of the building. On the main helipad was a police helicopter, an AS350B Squirrel. Its rotors were turning and the engine was firing up. As they were heading towards it, Mick's phone started ringing. 'Detective Greer!' Mick had to shout over the sound of the engine.

'It's Mackenzie, what's going on, Mick?'

'We're on our way to Canberra. Hauser told me that Benedict is plotting a siege on Parliament House!'

'Bloody oath…Are you sure this guy is legit?'

'No! But he knows he doesn't get out of police custody if he's making this up! One way or another, we'll find out!'

'Okay, how long will it take you to get there?'

'We should be there in twenty minutes! Can you authorise an assault squad?'

'Yes, I'll contact the AFP in Canberra. Tell them to send a squad to join you…Good luck, Mick. Let me know when you get there.'

Copy that!' Mick hung up the phone. Then, he and Ethan climbed into the chopper. Once they were secure, the chopper lifted off and headed into the night.

****

General Stanley and his team of mercenaries finally made it to Canberra after a three hour drive from Sydney. The van drove past a sign which had Canberra and then 5 Kilometres next to it. As they continued driving, the General took out his mobile phone to dial a number. 'Yes?' a voice answered.

'It's me. We just arrived in Canberra.'

'Good. No more communication until the target is secure,' said Karl Benedict.

'Copy that.' He hung up the phone. Then he

turned to the eight men sitting in the back. 'We're closing in boys. Time to load up.' The men acknowledged him and loaded their assault rifles. They were approaching the Parliament House. As they did so, the driver pulled into the service entrance. He was required to slow down and stop at the security checkpoint where a Parliament House Guard waited.

'I need to see some ID,' he said.

'Sure.' The driver rummaged about pretending to look for his ID. However, instead of presenting his license, the man pulled out a handgun with a suppressor on it. He fired a shot, killing the security guard. At that, he wound up his window and drove through the checkpoint. Finally, they parked in the underground visitor parking garage. General Stanley climbed out and opened the side door, allowing the eight men to pile out at the same time. They each carried Hecklar & Koch G36 assault rifles. Armed to the teeth, the men made their way into the building.

****

Charmaine Bradley was in her private study when the power went out. She'd been talking with the Deputy Prime Minister about his appointment to Prime Minister. They were confused as to what was going on. Jim Ross, the President's head of security came barging into the study. Charmaine looked up to see what was happening. 'What's the meaning of this?' she asked.

'Madam President. I've been informed there's been a security breach to the building,' said Jim.

'My God, what kind of security breach?' she asked.

'It's unclear, but we're going to do everything we can to protect you, Madam

President,' said Jim. At that, Charmaine gasped as she heard the distance sound of rapid gunfire. 'Ma'am, please stand up.' Jim and his team of bodyguards surrounded the President and the Deputy Prime Minister. While the President was their primary objective, the Deputy Prime Minister was technically next in line to the government, so they had to make sure he was safe also.

A few kilometres away from the Parliament House in Canberra, the New South Wales Police Force helicopter gently touched down nearby an Army Command Post that'd been set up by the Counter-Terrorism Squad. As the chopper landed, its cabin doors opened and Mick along with Ethan climbed out. They raced over to the command post where they were greeted by one of the senior officers. There were dozens of police vehicles and officers patrolling the area. Most of the streets leading in and out of that area had been sealed off by police. Police helicopters hovered overhead. 'Detective Senior Sergeant Mick Greer, this is my partner,

Detective Cooper, New South Wales Police Force,' said Mick, as they both presented their ID badges.

'I'm Major Cameron Dawson. Counter-Terrorism, Tactical Assault Group. Australian Army,' he said and they shook hands.

'What's the situation, Major?' asked Mick. They all stood around a large table with military gear and maps on it.

'We've got the entire residence surrounded. You guys are providing bodies on the harbour with patrol boats,' he began. 'Our specialist equipment reveals that there are at least eight or more armed hostiles inside. We've also detected the hostiles are holding hostages on the second floor of the residence.'

'Any communication from the hostiles?' asked Ethan. Major Dawson shook his head.

'Not yet. But they could be getting ready to make their demands, if they have any,' said the Major.

'Oh I'm sure they do. These guys are professional. They're not here for a suicide mission. They're doing this to make a statement,' said Ethan. 'We need to move in as soon as possible, Major. The President's life is at stake here.'

'I'm aware of that Detective Greer. But until we can be certain of the President's condition, we can't risk an entry that may result in casualties,' said the Major.

'Do you have a plan of entry?'

'We're coordinating an entry point as we speak. But it looks like the hostiles have every entrance point covered, so it could be a blood bath if we move in,' he said.

'I agree, Major. But these guys are professional hitmen. They've been hired to do one thing…Take out their target,' said Mick. The Major didn't know what to say after that. Then another officer came over to him.

'Sir, we're getting a live recorded message

from inside the residence. Looks like it's being streamed to all networks across the country,' said the officer. Both Major Dawson, Mick and Ethan turned and looked at the small TV monitor that was in the back of the van. On the screen was one of the hostiles, Major-General George Stanley.

'Good evening, Australians…Allow me to introduce myself. I'm Major-General George Stanley, of the former Royal Australian Army,' he began. The detectives were watching. 'I'm here tonight to inform you that this republic will no longer exist. I'm also informing you that I, Major-General George Stanley, will be taking over command of this government and this country, effective immediately,' he said. Ethan gasped at that. 'From now on, I will be the General of Australia. All decisions will go through me and through me alone,' he continued. 'Any attempt to retake this building will result in loss of life,' he threatened. 'This is

George Stanley, General of Australia, signing off.' At that, the screen went blank.

'Son of a bitch,' Ethan cursed.

'So looks like this guy just promoted himself to General and the head of government,' said Mick and Major Dawson nodded. Just then, the Major's phone started ringing.

'This is Major Dawson,' he answered. Both Ethan and Mick stood nearby and continued watching. 'With respect, Sir. I don't believe that's such a good idea. We could be risking the President's life as well as the other hostages,' said the Major.

There was another pause. 'Very well, as you wish, Sir. Thank you.' The Major hung up. 'That was the Governor. He's authorized a full assault on the residence. He wants this stopped. Let's suit up!' he ordered. He and his men began arming themselves. Ethan and Mick went back to their car and geared up with bullet-proof vests. As they were getting ready, Mick's phone started ringing.

'Detective Sergeant Greer,' he answered.

'It's me, I saw the live stream of the General's speech. What's happening, Greer?' it was Chief Inspector Anna Mackenzie.

'Boss, we're just about to move in on the residence.'

'Bloody oath. Are you sure that's a good idea?'

'Yes. And the Governor just authorised the operation.'

'Fair enough. Just be careful, Mick. I don't want to lose two of my best officers. That's an order.'

'Copy that. We're moving out.' Mick hung up and withdrew his handgun, a Glock 22. Ethan did the same. 'You ready?' he asked him. Ethan nervously nodded his head. Two Australian Army UH-60 Blackhawk helicopters flew overhead, providing aerial security.

****

There was a constant flash of gunfire within the Parliament House. The mercenaries were engaging in a gun battle with the President's private security. The President was safely secured inside her private study, along with Joe Parsons and Deputy Prime Minister Alistair Cohen. Jim was standing in front of the President with his gun raised and aimed at the door, waiting for the mercenaries to try and break in. 'This is insane,' said Charmaine, as she cowered behind Jim.

'Stay calm, Madam President. We're going to get through this,' Jim replied, trying to reassure her. 'I'm sure help is on the way.' He could hear more gunshots outside in the corridor. They were getting closer and the sound of bodies hitting the ground was quite audible. Just then, there was a loud explosion. This was followed by a brilliant flash of light. The explosion ripped through the large door. Both Jim and the

President fell to the ground. They were also blinded temporarily by the flash grenade that'd just entered the room. Within seconds of the explosion, the group of mercenaries swarmed in and immediately grabbed hold of the President. The mercenaries were victorious.

Inside the Parliament House, General Stanley was walking around the President's study. Charmaine Bradley, along with Joe Parsons and Jim Ross were on their knees with their arms tied behind their backs. They were being guarded by about four mercenaries, all armed with G36 assault rifles. General Stanley was currently talking on the phone. 'Yes Sir, you saw my speech?'

'Of course, you did well, General. Now you just have to convince the President to resign and officially take power,' said Karl. It was Karl Benedict.

'That shouldn't be a problem. I have several of her people at gunpoint,' he said.

'Good. Then get to it, General.' At that, the General hung up and grinned.

'You'll never get away with this, General,' Charmaine spoke out. The General stood there and chuckled. He then walked up to her and struck her across the face. The others cringed in empathy and went to help her as much as they could.

'Somehow I don't think that's possible…Madam President,' he said. He teased her with his gun.

****

Ethan Cooper and Mick Greer were following the team of officers from the Tactical Response Group. They were about to storm the Parliament House. They came up the steps that led them to the East Side entrance. This allowed the team to enter building. Thankfully, there were no signs of any hostiles in the area. The officers were equipped with night-vision goggles and enabled them to see perfectly without hindrance. Since Ethan and Mick didn't have that kind of equipment, they just followed close behind the officers. They began to get closer to the building. It was still in complete darkness. The lead officer could see through his night-vision that there were only two mercenaries patrolling the main entrance way of the House of Representatives chamber. He took out both of them with two silent shots. The officers were armed with Hecklar & Koch HK416 assault rifles. Now that the hostiles were down outside, the units moved forward, cautiously of course.

****

Making their way up the stairs from the main

entrance of the Parliament House was the twelve-man Counter-Terrorist assault unit. The lead officer had a tactical shield used to deflect bullets. They were getting ready to move in. General Stanley was standing next to the President. He had her at gunpoint and was holding onto her tightly. At that moment, everyone in the room was blinded by a brilliant flash of white light. A UH-60 Blackhawk helicopter came in low and it shone its spotlight in through the window. It was a blinding light, forcing the General to let go of the President in order to shield his eyes. Within a split second, the door to the study burst open. The Counter-Terrorism officers stormed the room, aiming their assault rifles at the hostiles. The helicopter backed off. Both Ethan and Mick entered the room with their weapons raised and fingers on the trigger. There was a sudden gun fight as they entered. The group of mercenaries open-fired. Several were taken out, but the others were taking cover behind objects in the study. As Ethan came in to take out a hostile, a bullet struck him in the shoulder. It hit him with force that he was knocked back slightly. 'Ethan!' Mick yelled. He stepped forward and started firing her gun. She took out several of the hostiles. Ethan was struggling to stand. He leaned against the wall, and gently lowered himself to the floor, grasping his wound. Blood was oozing from his shoulder. His vision was beginning to fade, but he fought to stay conscious. The gunfight soon came to an end as the tactical officers took out the remaining hostiles. All that remained, was General Stanley. They soon came to an impasse; General Stanley was holding the President in a choke hold and had pressed his gun to his head. He was preparing to kill him.

'Everybody back off!' General Stanley shouted. 'Back off, or I kill her!'

'Just take it easy!' Mick called out. 'Just

slowly put the weapon down and step away from the President!' he said. But the General wasn't having any of it.

'I'm not going to say it again…Drop your weapons!' he shouted, again. Mick was starting to worry. He was sweating.

'Just let the President go now and we can cut a deal,' said Mick, as he stepped forward slightly.

'This bitch is going down!' the General said. He lifted his gun and was about to pull the trigger. Within a split second, a shot was fired, and a bullet struck the General in the neck. He let go of the President and fell backwards to the floor. He was shot by one of the officers. At that, the assault unit moved in and immediately secured the President. Mick lowered his gun. Now that it was all over, Ethan passed out due to the significant blood loss from the gunshot wound he sustained. Mick came racing over to help him.

'I need a medic, now!' he shouted. At that, several paramedics came racing over to provide medical assistance.

193

Karl Benedict was not impressed. He'd just heard that the attempt to take out the President of Australia had failed. He was frustrated that the kill squad he'd hired failed to do their job when they seized the Parliament House. Karl wasn't happy that his operation was going downhill. He knew the Police were onto him and he had to get out of the country as soon as possible. He was sitting in the back seat of his limousine. The vehicle was driving and began to slow down as it approached its destination, Bankstown Airport. Bankstown Airport was roughly 26 kilometres from Sydney's CBD and operates numerous small aircraft, including business jets. Right now, Karl was on the phone. He was busy trying to figure out what went wrong. 'I'm disappointed in the General's work. He was supposed to kill her, then take over the country,' Karl snapped.

'I know. I don't know what happened. The good news is, it's all over.'

'Yes, well. I'm still pissed that bitch is still alive,' said Karl.

'What are you going to do now?' Karl paused for a moment before responding.

'There's nothing left for me to do here. I'm heading out of the country,' he said. 'Just make sure everything's handled on your end.'

'Of course, you can count on me, Mr. Benedict.' The female voice disconnected. After putting away his phone, he looked up to see where they were. They'd finally arrived at the airport. Karl's driver came over to open the door. He stepped out and grabbed his briefcase as he did. The glaring sun hit his face, so he quickly put on his sunglasses to protect his eyes. He nodded at his driver before making his way across the tarmac. Sitting there on the tarmac was Karl Benedict's private jet, a Gulfstream G650 business jet. Its engines were just starting up and the captain stood by the retractable stairway to greet Mr. Benedict. The captain smiled at Karl and took his briefcase. As Karl followed the captain onto the plane, he received a shock as he saw a familiar person sitting in one of the leather seats. 'What the bloody hell are you doing here?' he cursed. It was Shane Murphy.

'Just tying off some loose ends,' said Shane. He had a Glock 22 handgun aimed at him.

'You really think you're going to bring me down just by yourself, Murphy?' Shane didn't say anything.

'What makes you think I'm by myself?' he said, with sarcasm. 'Take a look out the window.' Shane nodded his head towards the door that was still open. Karl turned around and in the distance he could see several police cars driving at high speed towards them. They had their lights flashing and sirens going. 'They're coming for you, Benedict,' he said, still holding his gun at Karl. He turned back to face Shane.

'You fucking arsehole,' he cursed. 'I knew I shouldn't have hired you.' At that, the small plane was surrounded by half a dozen police cars and about the same number of police officers. Detective Senior Sergeant Mick Greer boarded the plane, along with two police officers. 'Karl Benedict, I'm placing you under arrest for the murder of two innocent people and the terrorist attack on the Sydney Opera House that resulted in the deaths of more than a hundred people,' said Mick. The officers went over to him and placed him in cuffs. 'Good work, Murphy,' he said, turning to Shane. 'Take this piece of shit away.' The officers took hold of Karl and escorted him off the plane.

Mick Greer was shocked that something like this had happened; the fact that a rogue group of military personnel attempted a siege on the Parliament House. Mick was in his office at the Ops Centre. It was just approaching 5am, and he was certainly finding it difficult to keep awake. Mick sat at his desk. The TV was on and it was showing a news report on the recent siege crisis at the Parliament House. It was stating that Counter-Terrorism units from the army stormed the Parliament House and recovered the President before she was publicly executed. All hostiles had been taken down in the process. As he sat there, he looked up to see his assistant poke her head in. 'Excuse me, Detective Greer. Anna Mackenzie is here to see you,' she said and Mick nodded.

'Thanks, Sonia. You're okay to go home now,' he replied, and she smiled with a hidden yawn. A few moments later, Anna Mackenzie stepped in. Mick stood up as she entered the office, and he buttoned his jacket. 'Well, it's been quite an interesting evening, wouldn't you say, Mick?' said Anna, showing herself to a seat.

'That's quite an understatement, Chief Inspector,' Mick replied, and sat back down.

'I take it Detective Cooper is doing okay?' she asked. Mick was quite surprised by that question.

'Yes, he's at the hospital in Canberra. He's currently undergoing surgery. He sustained a gunshot wound to the shoulder, but they say he's expected to make a full recovery,' Mick replied.

'Well, that's good to hear…I still can't believe that Birchall McClelland were behind all of this,' said Anna. There was a brief pause between them.

'I find that surprising to be honest,' he said. 'Considering the fact that we now know how Ethan was set up.' Anna looked at him, oddly.

'What do you mean? I thought BMC was behind it?'

'Oh yes, of course, they were. But we also discovered that BMC had a corrupt police detective working for them,' Mick began. He looked directly at Anna with a serious expression on her face.

'I see. And did you find out who it was?' she asked, curiously. Mick paused for a moment, as he played around with his laptop.

'Before the siege on the Parliament House, Shane Murphy came to me with some evidence which implicated BMC in this conspiracy,' said Mick. Anna didn't say anything. She just kept staring at him. 'The evidence was on a USB drive and in possession of Mitch Clark. That name ring a bell?' Anna shook her head. Of course, Mick knew she was lying. 'The USB also contained a string of recorded audio files,' he continued. 'One of the audio files was in fact a recording between Karl Benedict and the police informant,' Mick explained. Anna looked as if she'd just seen a ghost. It was like she knew what he was talking about.

'What are you implying?' she asked, softly.

'It turns out the informant BMC hired…Was you,' he said. At that, Anna started chuckling.

'Oh, you can't be serious, Mick? You really think I'm part of this conspiracy to overthrow the government?' she snapped. Mick kept his cool. He then turned his laptop around. It was an MP3 audio recording of a conversation. Mick pressed the play button. Anna sat there listening to the conversation. As soon as she heard it, she closed her eyes in shame. At that,

Mick paused the recording. Anna was sitting there in silence. She just had no words to say.

'We've also got documented proof from Hauser's laptop that he's been secretly messaging you through a secure chat log. I've got copies of the transcripts if you don't believe me,' he said, as he got out a folder. 'So, what I'd like to know is, how much did they pay you for betraying your own government?' he asked.

'This evidence will never be permissible through a court. I'll get a slap on the wrist,' she replied, with a sinister grin. Mick just smiled.

'That may be so, but you're still going down for this,' he said. At that, the office door opened, and two uniformed police officers stepped in. They stood behind Anna.

'Ma'am, please stand up,' said one of them. To start with, Anna didn't move. She just kept sitting there, staring at Mick with guilty eyes.

'Don't make this harder than it has to be, Anna,' said Mick. Finally, she slowly stood up.

The second officer placed handcuffs on her.

'Anna Mackenzie, I am arresting you on suspicions of conspiracy to commit murder, as well as conspiracy to overthrow the government,' the first officer began, 'you have the right to remain silent. If you do say anything, what you say can be used against you in a court of law. You have the right to consult with a lawyer and have that lawyer present during any questioning. If you cannot afford a lawyer, one will be appointed for you if you so desire,' said the officer. At that, they escorted her out of the office.

****

At Canberra Hospital, Ethan Cooper was recovering from the gunshot wound he sustained during the siege at the Parliament House. He'd just come out of surgery and was back in his room. It was early morning, sometime around 8:35am. The sun was well and truly up and it beamed through the blinds of the hospital room. Ethan slowly regained consciousness after his surgery. He was still a bit groggy, but that was from the anesthesia. To his surprise, Mick Greer was there. 'Hey. Welcome back to the land of the living,' he said, with sarcasm. Mick stood next to his bed and sipped on a large coffee. 'How are you feeling?' he asked.

'Ugh, like I've been shot,' he said, Mick just chuckled. 'What happened? Is the President okay?' he asked, getting excited. 'Relax, buddy. It's all over. The President's safe,' said Mick, taking a seat on the chair.

'Thank God. I don't remember much after General Stanley was shot.'

'That's because you passed out. Paramedics rushed you here after that,' said Mick.

'Is Dee okay?'

'Yes, she's fine. She's out in the hall waiting.'

There was a brief pause in the conversation, as Mick took a sip of his coffee. 'So, listen…Last night, the Chief Inspector was arrested…It turns out she was part of this conspiracy. She was also working with Karl Benedict,' he said. Ethan almost fainted, again.

'Bloody hell. How did you find that out?'

'We found the evidence on a USB drive. Mitch Clark, the bodyguard to President Bradley's husband had it. Our Tech Analysts went through a majority of the audio files Felicity recovered. One of them was conversation between Anna Mackenzie and Karl Benedict. They collaborated together.'

'Jesus…So, what's going to happen now?' said Ethan, with a croaky voice.

'Well, Mackenzie will be detained indefinitely until the court hearings, but she will likely end up going to prison,' said Mick. 'Also, Karl Benedict, the CEO of Birchall McClelland, was detained. Turns out he was the mastermind behind the whole thing. So, he'll likely end up going to prison for the rest of his life.'

'Good. The son of a bitch deserves it.' Mick slowly nodded. Ethan closed his eyes. He didn't say anything after that. Ethan had a TV in his room, and it was showing a news report on the recent siege at Parliament House.

'So…What are you going to do now?' said Mick. Ethan let out a deep sigh. Then he turned to look at Mick.

'Well, once I get out of this place, I'm taking a bloody holiday,' he said. Mick paused for a moment.

'That's a shame…I spoke with the Assistant Commissioner. He wants to give me Mackenzie's job as Chief Inspector,' said Mick.

'Well, I believe congrats is in order,' Ethan replied.

'Thank you…So, how does Detective Senior Sergeant sound to you?' Mick said. Ethan didn't say anything at first. Then he made a cheeky grin, and they both chuckled.

THE END

www.ingramcontent.com/pod-product-compliance
Lightning Source LLC
Chambersburg PA
CBHW071937150726
47999CB00001B/240